2/06

D1251896

FLAMESCAPE

Recent Titles by Gerald Hammond from Severn House

FINE TUNE
A RUNNING JUMP

FLAMESCAPE

Gerald Hammond

This first world edition published in Great Britain 1999 by
SEVERN HOUSE PUBLISHERS LTD of
9–15 High Street, Sutton, Surrey SM1 1DF.
This first world edition published in the USA 1999 by
SEVERN HOUSE PUBLISHERS INC., of
595 Madison Avenue, New York, NY 10022.

British Library Cataloguing in Publication Data

Hammond, Gerald, 1926-
    Flamescape
    1.   Photography - Fiction
    2.   Detective and mystery stories
    I.   Title
    823.9'14 [F]

    ISBN 0 7278 5501 8

Typeset by Palimpsest Book Production Ltd
Polmont, Stirlingshire, Scotland.
Printed and bound in Great Britain by
MPG Books Ltd, Bodmin, Cornwall.

FLAMESCAPE

Prologue

*J*enny Ambleton lay on her back because any other position hurt like hell. A small device in her hand was supposed to shoot a painkiller 'on demand' through a catheter into her wrist, but it seemed to do little more than heighten her sense of being trapped in a nightmare without having much effect on the pain from her burns.

And it did nothing to lighten her sense of impending doom, of a sword of Damocles hanging above her head. She had just begun to make her way in the world and now it seemed that she had lost her flat and everything she owned and there was every likelihood of her way being blocked. Possibly for ever. Possibly not. Not knowing was the worst of it. Disaster, she could have faced. Uncertainty could not be confronted.

On top of which, somebody unknown might or might not have tried to kill her, for some reason at which she could only guess. Her mind was beginning to wander again. Perhaps Bob could make some sense out of it. He seemed well able to do everything else. He had pulled her out of her burning flat like a cork from a bottle.

She took her finger off the plunger. Another patient had warned her, rightly or wrongly, that you could come out of the hospital hooked on morphine. That was one problem

1

she could do without. With the morbid fascination of one who picks at a scab, she turned her mind back. Where, she wondered, had it all begun?

It began, she thought, with the photographs.

One

It went back, she thought, to her seventeenth birthday, which seemed to be a hundred years ago but in fact was only two. There were other presents from the family, of course – some costume jewellery, make-up and a cheque from her father. He usually resorted to a cheque, which her mother said was the coward's way out. The mystery of a young daughter seemed to daunt him, as did the prospect of prowling a shop in search of a present for a young girl. Perhaps he feared being suspected of trying to please a young mistress, or of plain voyeurism. Mrs Ambleton was no help. A busy woman, bustling about on her do-good committees and fund-raisers, she had enough to do to choose a single present although she always insisted that they gave a present apiece.

But the major, the life-changing present, was from Dominic, her elder brother.

Dominic was already out in the world and earning, as a marine surveyor, a salary which caused their father to grumble non-stop at the way the younger generation had it all handed to them on a plate. Dominic had been reared in the digital age. He had been weighed at birth in kilos, measured his height in metric and been educated into the 'new maths' which so baffled his father. Dominic had grown up an electronic-gadget fiend. The needs of his profession qualified many of his extravagances to be purchased 'before tax', another cause of disquiet to Mr Ambleton. Photographic goods, in particular, were obviously essential to a marine surveyor, and Dominic had treated himself to the latest in digital cameras along with the printer and all the software to go with it. Even so, it was more than a surprise when, with no more than a casual "Happy birthday, Jen," he dropped into her lap a package containing the now superseded apple of his eye, a Pentax ME Super 35mm camera with a 50mm lens. The second package turned out to hold a large, 300mm telephoto lens.

Jenny would not have dreamed of 'looking a gift horse in the mouth', but her mother, who seemed to have known in advance of the intended gift, looked over Jenny's shoulder and said, "I thought you had another lens, one between those two."

Dominic shrugged. "I had a zoom lens. But I couldn't quite make the price of my new camera without trading it in. Sorry, Jenny."

"It doesn't matter a bit," Jenny said. "It's a lovely present. Thank you." She jumped up and gave her brother a kiss on the cheek. This was such a rare occurrence that he was dumbstruck until after she had left the room. Then he said, "I guess she liked it."

Jenny was still unsure whether it was a lovely present or not. Until that moment, photography had rather passed her by. Dominic had been the photographer in the family and two of her friends had inexpensive cameras, so that, without bothering to think about it, she had managed to accumulate a photographic record of any significant events in her life, mostly slipped between the pages of a large photo album although she had never yet got around to fixing any of them in place. But other people's photographs represented what the person holding the camera wanted to capture, which might not be at all what Jenny wanted to remember. When she came to think about it, she had been aware of a poignancy when life's sweetest moments slipped away and were gone. She had made sporadic attempts to keep a diary, but she was not very gifted with words and somehow her occasional attempts to record with due light and shade the subtleties of growing up had emerged with all the life and glamour of a suet pudding. The magic of those moments, she felt, had gone down the pan. She had them in her memory, but as time went by the edges blurred and the colours became dull.

The camera had a satisfyingly purposeful look. After a painstaking study of the instruction manual she spent a spare Sunday around the city's streets, parks and dockland, photographing whatever took her fancy.

The negatives and colour prints came back from the processing laboratory via the local chemist's shop. The results were a revelation. For the first time, she had captured something which she herself had identified as worthy of preservation and it would be with her for all time. Here were flowers, an old man on a bench, children at play, a boat sitting slantwise on the mud with a gull perched on its mast, all frozen in time at her behest and ready to be enjoyed again whenever the mood took her. Frozen, moreover, in the form and at the very instant which she, and not somebody else, wanted to remember. There were faults of exposure, of focus, of composition.

There was sometimes a lack of clarity due, she thought, to camera-shake; but she could see the faults clearly and she knew that she could learn from them.

She returned to the chemist's shop with the negative of one frame, a shot of a young child and a very hairy dog confronting each other over a large bone. For once her hand had been steady. Every hair was sharp and she had made use of all the subtleties of tone. She had a greater enlargement made and she bought a frame for it and hung it in her bedroom. Years later, it sold for a calendar.

Like most teenagers she had fallen into the habit of telling her parents as little as possible. She loved them, she supposed, in an abstract sort of way and she was sure that they loved her, but their wavelength was a different one and conversations with them led to seemingly endless discussions and left her feeling that her dreams had been violated. However, her newest dream was forced to emerge, blinking, into daylight a month after her birthday when she made preparations to go out on a weekday evening.

"New boyfriend?" her mother asked, any anxiety about her daughter's morals carefully overlaid by a girls-together coyness that set Jenny's teeth on edge.

"Unfortunately, no," Jenny said.

Mrs Ambleton abandoned coyness. "Then where are you going on a Tuesday evening?"

"To study."

"Study what? Who with?"

Jenny wore spectacles, black-framed to match her hair, and they gave her an owlish but somehow appealing expression. She regarded her mother over the top of them. "If you *must* know," she said with a great air

6

of world-weariness, "I'm taking an evening class in photography at the Tech."

It was probably only a passing enthusiasm and, while it lasted, much to be preferred to whatever girls got up to these days. Mrs Ambleton made one surreptitious phone call to the Technical College. She found that Jenny was indeed attending the photographic evening classes and let it go at that.

But the enthusiasm did not pass. After several months, when Jenny was still attending the Tech, now on two evenings a week, her mother felt moved to protest. She came home late one evening from a meeting of the local Neighbourhood Watch committee and, finding her daughter settled in the kitchen with a cup of tea and a photographic magazine, she poured a second cup and sat down at the other side of the Formica-topped table. "Darling," she said, "are you sure you can spare the time from your *proper* studying? After all, this *is* an important year."

Jenny frowned, turning at bay. "I'm not all that interested in exam results."

"But the university . . ."

"And nothing would drag me to university. I want to study photography. It may not convey the reflected status you're hoping for. You may not be able to refer airily to 'my daughter the gynaecologist', that sort of thing – but it's what I want to *do*. There's a one-year full-time course at the Tech and I've already got all I need to get into it. In fact, I've already been accepted."

"But, darling, a *photographer*?"

"Why not? Mr Belfrage says I'm a natural. He says that I have a good sense of composition and a better grasp of the technicalities than most of the men. He says that I could make it."

Mr Belfrage, who was a weedy man in middle age with a goatee beard and spots, had indeed said that and more. The fact that shortly thereafter he made a serious pass at Jenny, which was indignantly rejected, was irrelevant. They both knew that he had, for once, been sincere.

"That's all very well," Mrs Ambleton said later to her husband, "but is it a suitable job for a girl?"

"More suitable than most," Jenny's father said. "And better than being on the other end of a camera." At the back of his mind, half recognised, was the unworthy thought that if Jenny put off going to university until she became a mature student, parental contribution might no longer be a requisite; the demands on his pocket would be less heavy and less enduring and perhaps he would be able to afford the small yacht for which he had always hankered. He was ashamed of the thought, but it was there all the same.

"What," demanded Mrs Ambleton, "is that supposed to mean?"

Jenny's father was a shy man and disinclined to provoke his wife who, placid though she might seem, had a strength of character which always managed to intimidate him. "Well," he said, "I wouldn't want to see her photograph on Page Three."

"But you wouldn't mind seeing her name under a girlie photograph, credited – if that's the word – with having taken it?"

"Not particularly," Mr Ambleton said after a moment's thought. "Provided that it was a good photograph."

They fell to arguing about what 'good' meant in that context.

*　　*　　*

8

It was not to be expected that those few words would be an end to the matter, but both of Jenny's parents had more than enough to occupy their minds and it was a relief, on the whole, to find that the second of their offspring now seemed to be settling her own future with only minimal and comparatively short-term financial assistance. Jenny, to their relief, after a truculent youth and rebellious teens, at last seemed happy and fulfilled. For Christmas she asked, and nagged her father until she was given, contact lenses. Spectacles got in the way of a viewfinder.

More than a year after the original gift of the camera, in the late autumn when Jenny was nearing the middle of her course and he could see the yearned-for yacht coming almost within his grasp, Mr Ambleton nevertheless felt obliged to have another word with his daughter. On an evening of weather too wild for her to be out with her camera, he cornered her in the sitting room where she was established in a shabby but comfortable chair with a book and a glass of shandy.

"You know," he said, "that we always hoped you'd go to university and qualify for a worthwhile career?"

Jenny looked amused. She listened for a moment to rain being thrown against the window. "And then turn it up to become a mother and housewife to some life-partner?"

"That's always a risk," he admitted. "But we wouldn't have grudged you the education and there would have been the chance of meeting a better quality of—" he swallowed. *Husband*, it seemed, had become a politically incorrect, almost a dirty word. "—life-partner. Photography is a job of sorts but I don't see it leading anywhere."

9

"It's led David La Chapelle somewhere. And Helmut Newton."

He looked blank. "I've never heard of either of them."

"But then you're a thousand years behind the times," she pointed out. "You've heard of David Bailey? Lord Snowdon? Ditto Lichfield?"

Mr Ambleton avoided the errors of pointing out that these were men or that Jenny had no royal connection. "I don't think photographers are well paid," he said. "You'll never make money at it."

"I expect I'll survive."

Fate seemed determined to prove Mr Ambleton at fault. Two evenings later, Jenny was cycling home from an evening class when a fire appliance swept by her, followed by a second and then a third, with the full drama of flashing lights and sounding klaxons. On an impulse, she turned her bike and followed. The road being downhill, the traffic thin and the wind behind her, she had no difficulty keeping them in sight for half a mile by which time a glow in the sky beckoned her onward.

The fire was at a modern single-storey building set back from a main road out of the city behind its own yard. The fire seemed to be mostly confined to a collection of discarded cardboard boxes and other packaging in the yard. A neon sign, not lit, read 'Westerlink'. An early shower had gone past but it had left behind a brisk wind which was whipping up the flames. There was little doubt that it would soon burn out or come under control, leaving behind little more than blackened brickwork and some ash to blow in the wind, but while it lasted it was a pictorial opportunity illuminated by movement and drama. Jenny had the camera in her bag and a fast black-and-white film in the camera. At that time, she had not thought beyond a few good enlargements for the end-of-course exhibition. She climbed precariously onto a nearby skip and took several shots of the flames and sparks leaping higher than the roof. She added the electronic flash unit, which had been a birthday present, and captured the avid faces of the few spectators who had had time to gather and of the ordered activity of the firefighters, the snaking hoses and magically suspended shafts of water.

The flames surrendered to foam and water and began to die.

Jenny found that the skip, which she had climbed easily in the heat of the moment, was less easy to dismount safely and modestly in the gale which was now gusting ferociously. A man who had been watching the scene from nearby held up his hands to her. He was slightly overweight but he was well dressed and looked respectable, so Jenny first handed down her bag and then let him take her hands and help her down.

"Thanks," she said. Something had been puzzling her. "Why did they send three fire engines to a cardboard-box fire?" she asked him.

"That would be automatic," the man said. He pointed to some empty drums stacked at the end of the yard. "They make marine electronics here, radars, echo-sounders, satellite navigation and all that. They use a lot of radioactive materials. Any alarm would be answered by three appliances, minimum."

Jenny thanked him again. She took the camera and flash out of her bag, fitted the long-focus lens, steadied the now heavy apparatus on a corner of the skip and took several shots of the drums with their stencilled symbols against a background of firemen and hoses and the signboard of the factory. A fireman came and chased her away. It was too far for her flash to have much effect, but at a slow shutter-speed, supplemented by street lighting and the floodlights on the fire appliances, she should have one or two printable frames.

Cycling back up the hill towards home, Jenny thought hard. Her route took her not far from the ancient building housing the foremost of the local papers, perhaps her most likely employer when she should complete her photography course. Now might be a good time to make a first approach. The paper came out in the mornings, so surely there would be someone there at night? Moreover, the wind was making cycling difficult and possibly dangerous. She turned off and pedalled up a side street into a square dominated by the Victorian pile.

The building, a masterpiece of hideous detail lovingly executed in an ugly red sandstone, was still illuminated and the glass doors were moving in the wind. With the help of a large and elderly uniformed doorman, Jenny managed to manoeuvre her bicycle through the doors and into a large hall hung with framed copies of the front page on historic occasions. (In the view of the editors of the *Tidings*, history was mostly made when the paper scooped all its rivals.) The sound of machines could be heard from somewhere in the building but it was a haven of calm after the wind outside.

The doorman was helpful. He listened to Jenny's demand to see someone about a story with photographs and then retired behind a desk to use a telephone. "Someone will be down in a minute," he said. "They'll take you to Mr Jessop."

"And Mr Jessop is?"

"Night editor." The doorman seemed surprised that anyone could be ignorant of the fact. He promised to guard her bicycle and camera bag with his life.

Jenny thanked him. While she waited in silence but for the distant machines, she busied herself in winding back and extracting her film. At last a grubby and tired-looking woman came to lead her through endless corridors and up many stairs to where, in a corner of a large but otherwise empty office, two men were conferring in a localised pool of light in front of a computer terminal.

One of them turned to meet Jenny. He was bald and, to Jenny's young eyes, looked as old as the hills but he exuded energy. "You have something for us, Miss . . . ?"

"Ambleton. Jenny Ambleton. You know about the fire at Westerlink's?"

He nodded. "We heard about it, but too late to get anyone there. Is that all?" Jenny was left in no doubt that, though he was polite, he was anxious to get back to his study of a pasted mock-up of a page.

"I have photographs," she said.

His interest flickered for a moment. Then he shrugged. "The factory was undamaged except by smoke. Somebody phoned in a report. That's enough for today and by tomorrow it'll be dead. I'm not going to tear the paper apart for a photograph. We have to get the paper *out*, not just written."

On the point of turning away defeated, Jenny said, "Did you know that there were radioactive materials there?"

Suddenly she had Mr Jessop's full attention. "You're sure?" he asked.

Gerald Hammond

"I have photographs." She sent up a silent prayer that the light had been adequate, that she had found the right settings in the dimness.

The younger man spoke up. "We have time, just. We could hold over the feature about the garden competition until tomorrow."

"Right," said Mr Jessop. "Where's your film?"

Jenny held the cassette out to him but the other man took it and hurried out.

From a bunch of papers, Mr Jessop produced one on which a small rectangle of print gave the bare facts about the fire. "Can you type?" he asked.

"Only hunt-and-peck."

"And I don't suppose you've any experience of writing up a story?"

"Not yet," Jenny said. "I'm studying photography, not journalism."

"Study both. You'll be less of a drag on the market."

Jenny thanked him but she felt a momentary depression. She was never quite at ease with the spoken word, cultivating a levity of manner to cover her uncertainties; and between herself and the written word there seemed to be a scrambler, so that what left her pen as clear and coherent arrived on the paper barely literate. If she could not make it with her camera, she decided, she would just have to do without it.

The other man returned. "Charlie said thirty minutes. I told him twenty."

Jenny was stunned at the idea that anyone could blast her negatives through development and drying and even make enlargements to that sort of timescale, but Jessop nodded. The exchange seemed to be routine. "Take Miss

14

Ambleton into my room and re-cast the Westerlink story. Mr Hines will look after you," he told Jenny. He went back to arranging clippings in page format and repeating the result on his monitor.

Mr Jessop's room was a cluttered cubicle screened off from the big office. Hines sat down at an already lit computer console. Jenny was left to perch against a cluttered desk. "Headline," he said. "How about 'Radiation Scare'?"

"I don't think anyone was scared," Jenny said.

"They will be when we've done our stuff." He typed the two words.

Jenny had thought that the short paragraph already typeset had said it all, but she was now permitted to witness an experienced journalist making bricks without straw. Prodded by questions, she revealed everything that she could remember about the scene, and her recollections were extended by the use of intelligent inference. The single paragraph had been extended a dozen times when her tired-looking guide from earlier joined them. Mr Jessop must have issued some instructions, because she had a short list of phone calls to lay before Mr Hines.

"Fire Service playing down any danger but unable to give any reason for the outbreak," Hines said, studying the list. "Nobody available for comment at the Town Hall, the Atomic Energy Authority and so forth."

"That's a pity," Jenny said.

Hines drew his breath in sharply at this heresy. "Not a pity at all. Almost as good as a refusal to comment which itself is almost as good as an admission. The last thing we need is for some expert to tell us that it was a non-event." Mr Hines added a couple of lines to his story, enlarged the headline and took off a print.

Back in the big office Mr Jessop already had a set of Jenny's prints at hand. He handed her an envelope with her negatives. "Charlie was quite impressed," he said. "He had to use some intensifier on the shots of the drums, but he says you did very well in the light available. Very dramatic, the sharp drums with the smoke and firemen out of focus in the background. We'll buy them. A hundred?"

Things were moving rather fast for Jenny. "Pounds?" she asked.

"I'm not talking pesos."

Jenny had set her heart on a zoom lens which would nicely fill the gap between her 50mm lens and the telephoto. Even second-hand, a hundred would not cover the example in a local camera shop. "A hundred and fifty," she said. "And you print my credit with the photographs."

Mr Jessop blinked at her, pursed his lips and tutted. Jenny's heart sank. She had killed the deal out of avarice. But Jessop scanned quickly through the story. "You drive a hard bargain, young lady. But very well. One-fifty it is. Bring us anything else you come across." He turned away. Jenny saw that he was already arranging her story and photographs on his own computer terminal.

Mr Hines produced a printed form which she signed. "Your cheque will come through at the end of the month," Hines said.

Jenny thanked him politely and, without quite knowing how, found herself back in the entrance hall. She borrowed the doorkeeper's phone and called home.

"Where on earth have you been?" her father demanded. "Your mother's going frantic."

Jenny tried to keep her sigh silent. Her mother, always calm and imperturbable in her charitable and political activities, was inclined to go frantic at the drop of almost anything when one of her family was involved. "Tell her I'm all right. I've been selling some photographs to the local rag. And now I'm tired and I see the rain's on again and I've gone out of my way and I want my bed and I don't really much fancy the cycle ride in this weather and against this wind. Could you come and fetch me? Pretty please?"

Mr Ambleton protested. He had been about to go to his own bed. It would mean folding down the rear seats to make room for the bicycle. And the car had just been washed. But the outcome was never in doubt. Jenny travelled home in comfort, hugging herself.

* * *

In the morning, Jenny rose in a hurry and caught the paper as it came through the letterbox. Her story and photographs had been too late for the first four pages, which had already been set up and ready to roll if not already in print, but she had been given a good splash on Page 5 and her name duly appeared under each photograph. The family was filled with admiration and Jenny glowed. She had, she thought, handled the business as if she had been negotiating all her life. Obviously she was cut out for the life of a freelance.

Others were not so impressed. On the following Saturday, when Jenny returned from a cycling trip in search of further subject matter (which had produced nothing more interesting than a motorist being breathalysed), she found a visitor waiting for her, nursing a crocodile briefcase. Her mother, having already decided that the man was respectable, introduced him as Mr Dan Mandible and left them alone together in the dining room. They settled on opposite sides of the dark oak table, in the matching oak chairs with red leather seats which had been in the family for as long as Jenny could remember.

"I saw your photos in the papers," Mr Mandible said. "All things considered, they're good. You chose the right aspects and made good, newsworthy pictures out of them. I expected to meet somebody older. Not your fault," he added quickly as Jenny looked ready to apologise, "and time will put that right, but I was hoping that you would turn out to be a professional, a freelance."

"That's exactly what I'd like to be, when I finish the photography course at the Tech, but I suppose I'll end up as a wage-slave on some local paper."

"Ah." Mr Mandible was a small, slim man in his sixties with silver hair, gold-rimmed spectacles hooked over tiny ears and a smile which seemed to skip over his full-lipped mouth and to arrive first at a pair of very blue eyes. He wore an immaculate suit of rather a loud pattern – in the hope, Jenny thought, of making himself look bigger. "Perhaps," he said, "I'd better tell you about myself. I retired two years ago after many years of working for Reuters, mostly in the Middle East. I'd reached retiring age anyway, but a mild heart attack forced the issue. And now, I'm as fully recovered as I'll ever be. Most men delight in retirement, but it's not my scene at all. I'm accustomed to being busy, you see, and I've no interest in hobbies, no physique for sport and I don't even have the hand-eye coordination for golf or bowls. I'm bored out of my mind. Can you understand that?"

Jenny was immediately sympathetic. Her mother had always said that Jenny's threshold of boredom was very low. "I can understand it very easily," she said. "One thing that I don't do well is nothing."

Mr Mandible considered the comment until he made sense of it. "Well put!" he said doubtfully. "So I thought that I might get back into the only thing I know and enjoy, and act for a strictly limited number of writers and photographers in journalism and the media. Nothing too arduous – I want to live to a very old age – and only the ones I think are going to be good."

Jenny felt immensely flattered yet at the same time flustered. "I don't think I'm ready for an agent yet," she said. "And for all that I could earn at first it wouldn't be worth your while and I couldn't really spare ten per cent to somebody else."

"Fifteen per cent," Mr Mandible corrected her. "Let me ask you one thing. I got your address from the paper but, quite rightly, they wouldn't tell me how much they paid you."

"There's no secret about it," Jenny said. "At least, I don't think there is. A hundred and fifty pounds."

"You signed an agreement?"

"Yes."

"May I see it?"

"I don't see why not," Jenny said. "It was only a standard printed form, giving them permission to publish. Are you feeling all right?" she added as Mr Mandible closed his eyes, apparently in pain.

"I'm all right," he said. "And you?"

"I feel fine," Jenny said, surprised.

"Let me have a look at that form of agreement and I'll tell you if you should feel fine or not."

"Hang on a moment." She went through to her bedroom and brought back the form.

Mr Mandible studied it for a moment. "You were robbed," he said. "You sold them all rights to the photographs. On the face of it, you did well. Those drums were empty and had been put out for collection by a contractor who was running a little late. At the moment the experts are all saying that even if all the radioactive material in the factory had blown across the city, nobody would have received more radiation that he might get in a day from a luminous wristwatch."

"Fine. That's all very reassuring. But that assurance wouldn't stop a go-ahead journalist from blowing up a storm. The *Tidings* is busily selling your photographs all over the world. They've already been seen on Japanese television. A fire near radioactive material is news. It smacks of Chernobyl, however the experts try to play it down. Added to which, although it was probably caused by a couple of school-kids having a secret smoke, there's a whisper going around that the fire may have been started deliberately and that it isn't the first one in the area, so the media are stockpiling photographs for when the real story breaks. The *Tidings* must be doing very nicely, thank you."

Jenny sat and seethed for a moment. "And I was thinking of asking them for a job," she said bitterly at last.

"You can make more as a freelance, with a little help from me."

"I wouldn't work for them now if they were the last

paper on earth, not as a wage-slave. They can buy my work if they want to. I don't take kindly to being ripped off." That thought was followed by another. There was no doubt that Mr Mandible, with his experience, could have driven a far better bargain than she had obtained by herself. On the other hand, it would be possible for an agent to do absolutely nothing and still collect a percentage of her earnings for ever. Having been stung once, Jenny was in no hurry to give her trust again. "You can be my agent," she said, "but on a trial basis for the first year. And my first instruction is that you screw those bastards whenever you can."

"That will be my pleasure. The first year will be a lot of work and not much reward for either of us," Mr Mandible said. "But I have faith in you and I have faith in myself." He produced a typed form of agreement from his briefcase and added a paragraph in neat script. "Read it over carefully this time," he told her, "and consider the implications."

"As my agent," Jenny said, "you read it and point out the significant bits."

Half an hour later, they each had a signed copy of the agreement.

"Now that I am officially your agent," he said, "I'll hand out a few words of advice. Do you mind?"

"Of course not, Mr Mandible. I need all the advice I can get."

The smiling eyes beamed at her while his mouth remained still. "The first word is to call me Dan. Everybody else does. I may be just about old enough to be your grandfather, but I've never taken to my surname. Mandible. The lower jaw. I never did find out what some remote ancestor of mine did to be credited with the name. All right?"

"All right . . . Dan."

"Good. Next. I'll soon have you paying income tax and VAT. Keep proper accounts. Note down everything you spend which could possibly be considered a business expense, going back to the very beginning. Keep all receipts. Get somebody to teach you elementary book-keeping. Believe me, it's a lot less work noting your expenditures down in the right column from the start than trying to sort out a muddle later with a disbelieving tax inspector breathing down your neck.

"Go out and about. Until we build up regular contacts for you, you'll be dependent on selling shots that you can find for yourself. Like the fire. Look for them. Develop an instinct for when something's brewing. Learn to recognise the signs. When it comes, capture it quickly before it goes away.

"Lastly, never, ever, part with a negative. And index everything, starting with the first shot you ever took. Get names when you can. Because you never know. Tomorrow, you snap young Ezekial Snodgrass walking on the beach with some girl. Twenty years later, the name rings a bell."

"As it would," she said.

"As it would," he agreed. "But the point is that Snodgrass is now an MP and Privy Councillor and he's involved in a sex scandal. He tells Parliament that the woman came and spoke to him and he never saw her before in his life. But your photograph says different. It's worth real money to the tabloids . . . if you can find it. So index everything by name and subject and date and place and anything else you can think of. It will be a lot of work but you'll thank me some day. Once again, it's easier to write up an index as you go along than to search through tens of thousands of negatives, years later.

"And now, before I go, show me all the photographs you've ever taken. The emulsion may be gold instead of silver."

Two

D an Mandible had been so earnest in his encouragement to get out and about, patrolling the area for newsworthy subjects, and so optimistic about her future earnings that Jenny emptied the saving account which housed the remains of her Christmas and birthday presents over many years and sold her bicycle in order to scrape together a down payment on a motor scooter. A friend at college gave her some introductory instructions and Jenny spent most of her free moments, L-plate to the fore, circling and criss-crossing the city streets and such country roads as were within scootering reach. Memorisation of the Highway Code was added to her other studies. Her mother daily prophesied disaster under the wheels of a juggernaut driven by some mad Continental who had forgotten which side of the road to follow, but Jenny proved a competent rider and passed her test in the spring at the first attempt. Looking to the future, however, she persuaded her mother to stump up for a series of driving lessons. With Mrs Ambleton's eternal expectation of disaster, it was the softest touch of Jenny's life so far.

Before there could be any prospect of a change from two wheels to four, there were other tribulations to be overcome. In particular, the insurance companies had proved strangely reluctant to give even the minimal cover required by law to a young female scootering student with no history of no-claims at less than exorbitant terms, and the payments on her scooter were a serious drain on her income. She was determined not to turn to her father for help because, despite his many virtues, he was given to the vice of saying, "I told you so." Before disaster quite struck, she gained a respite by coming across, first, a derailed goods engine and, the following week, a major bust-up between rival gangs outside the football ground, nearly herself becoming embroiled in the fracas in the process. (This latter, though only moderately remunerative at the time, proved a valuable source of income for years to come. As the case trailed on through the courts, first the police, then the defendants and later the Football Association and several fan clubs all demanded ever more prints for the purpose of identifying and penalising the hooligans. These Jenny was only too pleased to furnish although, for once, she preferred not to have her name associated with them for fear of possible reprisals.)

At first, Jenny had had doubts about her relationship with Dan Mandible. It was true that he had driven a better bargain with the local press for these few items than she would have dared to demand for herself, but there was little sign of activity on his part. Then, just as bankruptcy or, worse, repossession of the cherished scooter seemed inevitable, he sold to an up-market magazine one of her early shots, of three old men sitting on a park bench and looking with wistful eyes at the departing back of a girl in a short and clinging skirt. Insolvency retreated for another week or two.

Shortly before Christmas, she discovered that Dan had not been altogether idle. He was on the phone to her. "Do you have a passport?"

"Yes. Why?"

"How would you like a fortnight in the Caribbean?" he asked her.

"Is this work or an invitation?"

He sounded amused. "If I were twenty years younger and you were twenty years older, it would be a proposition. As it is, it's work, hard work and quite a lot of it, but you should come back with a worthwhile sum in wherever young girls carry their money these days. It's on a cruise ship, doing a two-week cruise over Christmas and the New Year. They usually carry two photographers but one of them's broken his ankle and he can't possibly stand on one leg and a pair of crutches in a moving ship while he takes photographs. Apparently the other man can't cope on his own, I don't know why. They have a replacement but he isn't available until early January. Your air fare's paid for you, you get free cabin and food and use of photographic equipment and facilities but after that you're in business for yourself. I won't even charge you commission except on any sellable photographs of your own that you bring back with you. Do you want it or don't you?"

Jenny thought quickly. She would miss a family Christmas, which was definitely on the plus side, because a family Christmas entailed church attendances, too much rich food and a constant need for enforced jollity just when she would rather have screamed aloud and escaped to the pictures. All this could be expected to take place in regrettably seasonable weather – not, according to the long-term forecasts, snow, which might have been acceptable and even worthy of her photographic attention, but drizzle and wind. The job would fit nicely into the vacation.

"I want it," she said. "You'll never know how much. When do I go?"

"Tonight. The ship sails from Fort Lauderdale tomorrow afternoon."

"Wow!"

The attitude of the family showed a delicate balance between regret at her impending absence over the festive season and envy of her good fortune, but they cooperated willingly in helping her to select and pack suitable clothing, find her passport, acquire a few dollars for immediate expenses and confirm her flight booking. Her mother ensured that she had at least a minimum of jewellery for formal occasions but was unable to lend her a dress which would not have hung in festoons about her slimmer daughter.

Jenny's father, driving her to the airport, gave her a lecture about the dangers to be encountered under a tropical moon. She explained to him – gently, because she was a kindly girl – that the same dangers could be encountered and circumvented as easily under a British drizzle. He seemed surprised and mildly shocked at the revelation, which confirmed her impression that her father had led rather a sheltered life. He was a shy and slightly reclusive man who made an adequate living from dealing in old books.

No time later, as it seemed, she found herself cramped into an uncomfortable seat in a Boeing 767 high above the Atlantic. She managed to distort herself into a position in which the major components of her body were supported and slept for most of the journey, woke with a sore neck and a numb posterior, suffered (in both senses of the word) the delays built into the American immigration system and took a taxi to the docks.

The ship, to her relief, turned out not to be one of the monsters of the ocean which were to be seen in Fort Lauderdale but a rather smaller vessel, catering for the top end of the market but carrying less than a thousand passengers. All the same, Dan Mandible's prognostication of 'hard work and lots of it' was not wide of the mark. Jenny and her temporary partner, one Jonas Briggs, were expected to photograph every couple or group on every occasion, such as coming aboard and the various games and functions that filled the passengers' evenings and whole days at sea. They were also required to process their own and the passengers' films, exhibit sample prints, take orders and deliver the finished work. Another of their tasks was to supply the passengers with films, camera batteries and, when requested, good advice.

One penance Jenny was usually spared. It was soon clear why Jonas would never have been able to cope on his own. He was a middle-aged man with a surly manner and disposition who never went ashore but spent his free moments benefiting from the duty-free supplies in the various bars. Only rarely and in closely controlled circumstances was he allowed to meet and photograph the passengers. He would never have been tolerated in his position but for his counterbalancing talents. He was a dab hand at the processing and he had a cast-iron stomach. Jenny's few turns at operating the equipment, partly in darkness, in a badly ventilated little closet in the bows of the ship where every pitch or roll was magnified, were seeming eternities of seasickness and other discomforts. She was only able to do the work at all because the equipment was similar to some on which she was being taught at the Technical College. (Jonas said that it was all being replaced shortly as part of the ship's modernisation programme and Jenny, on an impulse, asked him to help her to acquire it. Jonas promised to do his best and she was sure that he had forgotten all about it two minutes later.)

They soon settled into a routine. Jonas undertook the processing and managed the complex paperwork which kept track of their financial entitlement, while Jenny took the photographs, exhibited the results on the noticeboard which occupied a whole wall outside the dining rooms, took orders, delivered the prints and returned developed and printed films to their owners, occasionally pacifying dissatisfied clients who had been fooled by the bright, tropic light into overexposing their films.

Her cheerful manner and youthful good looks made her popular, especially with the younger officers. She was soon gratified to discover that her out-of-pocket expenses were almost literally nil because there seemed always to be a young man in tropical whites at her elbow, eager to pay for her refreshments or to escort her ashore. In daytime, a tropical cruise made few demands on her wardrobe, so she was able to devote some of her available spending money to a short red evening dress complete with shoes and accessories, suitable for evening wear by one of her black hair and vivid colouring, from the ship's boutique.

Whenever she was not hurrying between venues and taking endless portraits of couples entering or leaving the various functions, or standing behind the three feet of counter which served as the photographic shop, Jenny was free to mingle with the passengers and make use of the ship's facilities. At the Christmas and New Year's Eve parties she performed her photographic duties but also danced until she was exhausted. After the gloom of midwinter Britain, the sunshine went to her head more potently than the ever-present rum punch and wherever they met land the smell of flowers was just as intoxicating. Under the tuition of a handsome but respectful junior officer with curly hair and a French accent which made her toes curl, she experienced snorkelling in the Dominican Republic, windsurfing in Puerto Rico, both parascending and jet-skiing in Montserrat and kisses on a beach in the Bahamas under that same tropical moon against which her father had warned her. They swore undying love and forgot about each other almost as soon as the cruise was over.

For her personal amusement she photographed shipboard life, venturing into places to which the passengers never penetrated and capturing dolphins in the bow wave and crew at work, and also such unusual occasions as when, passing through the wash of a larger vessel, the ship had spilled half the contents of the open air pool among the passengers. At Jonas's suggestion she mounted those shots with the others and copies sold well.

As the cruise went by she became aware of faces that gave her a sense of *déjà vu*. Sometimes these were encountered on deck or across the dinner table, sometimes glimpsed through the viewfinder of her camera. Usually she managed to pin them down as minor celebrities seen on television – a footballer, a news-reader and a jockey –

or to chance resemblances to people at home, but on one of the days spent entirely at sea she headed back through a lounge after passing a quiet hour with her own camera in search of the unusual, the photogenic or the bizarre. A man was sitting alone, looking out at the reflected sunshine dancing over a placid sea. He was tall and very slightly overweight, with a square jaw, a determined nose and an air of restrained energy. His dark hair was touched with a distinguished streak of grey. Other passengers were wearing shorts and brightly patterned shirts but he was dressed, correctly but unnecessarily, in a blazer, flannels and a shirt with what looked like a club tie. She had seen him several times on the cruise and had been sure that she had seen him somewhere else. Now a wink of gold from his watch and cuff links reminded her of a redder glint in the light of flames.

She caught his eye and smiled. "May I join you?"

His eyebrows went up and he hesitated for a fraction of a moment. "Yes, of course. Delighted." He sketched the preliminary to rising as she took the seat opposite.

"I think we've met before," she said. "But you don't remember, do you?"

Where most other men would have wondered aloud how they could ever have forgotten such an encounter, he avoided paying the easy compliment. He smiled. "I'm afraid not," he said.

"It was at the scene of the fire at Westerlink's. I was taking photographs from on top of a skip and you were kind enough to help me down. And you tipped me off that the drums had contained radioactive material, so I got my start by selling the photographs to the *Tidings*."

He smiled, showing white teeth and some pink gum, but

they were his own teeth and his own gums. "Now I remember. The papers made a silly fuss about a non-existent radiation danger and your photographs accompanied every story. You must have made a fortune."

"Unfortunately not," she said. "I was ripped off. The *Tidings* made the fortune. But I have an agent now, so it won't happen again."

"And now you're the ship's photographer?"

"Only for this trip. The usual man fell down a companionway and broke something. I'm still a student."

"Of photography?"

"Yes."

Her feet were tired, the ship was rolling slightly despite the stabilisers, there were no particular calls on her time for the moment and he was a good listener. Jenny stayed in her seat and a Filipino waitress brought her a coffee. She found herself drawn out, making amusing anecdotes out of her efforts to establish herself as a freelance photographer.

Her companion chuckled at all the right moments. He looked up suddenly as a woman arrived at their corner and said, "Here's my wife, come to see that we don't get into any mischief. I don't think I know your name."

"Jenny Ambleton. And I don't know yours," Jenny said. She shook hands with a lady who, although past the first bloom of youth, was still to be considered attractive. She was thin, just managing to be slender rather than gaunt. The red hair colour was no more natural than the other carefully applied make-up. Jenny, trained to appreciate the visual and with eyes becoming wise to nuances of style, decided that the other woman's clothes were expensive, appropriate and chosen to make the most of a figure beginning to run to seed. Beneath the skilful make-up were sharp features and slightly protuberant eyes, cleverly camouflaged by counter-shading. The eyes studied Jenny in detail. The man's slight hesitation before inviting Jenny to join him was explained.

"Ships that pass in the night," the man agreed. He began to tell his wife the story of the fire at Westerlink's. Jenny looked at her watch. Time had shot away from her and she was overdue at a rehearsal for the fancy dress parade. "You'll have to excuse me," she said. She got up. "Duty calls. I hope we meet again some time," she added politely.

"I'm sure we will," said the man, half rising. His good manners, Jenny noticed, were only skin deep.

She began to walk away, but on a friendly impulse turned and raised her camera.

The couple watched her departing figure. The woman might have been envying her youth but the man showed annoyance. When she was out of sight, he said, "I hope we bloody well don't. Meet again, I mean. This has been the purest bad luck."

The woman yawned. "She's already photographed us together a dozen times. Does once more matter?"

He shrugged. "I think it might. All these shots taken on spec will be chucked away with the rest of the garbage. But she seemed to take that one for herself. If it doesn't appear on the board, we'll know. I don't like the idea of it lying in limbo, waiting to appear at the wrong moment."

"Maybe you should offer to buy the negative."

He shook his head decisively. "Bad idea. That would fix it in her mind. We'll just have to delay things."

The woman pursed her thin lips and her eyes narrowed. "Even longer? I am not going to wait for ever, you know."

"I'm afraid so. Have patience," he said soothingly. "We'll have to wait until memory fades. We wouldn't want that girl seeing Sibyl's photograph in the paper beside mine. That would certainly bring the whole story out."

"I suppose so." The woman sighed. "How long?"

"We'll see how it goes."

"All we need now is for your wife to be waiting at the dockside."

The man gave a harsh bark of laughter although he did not look amused. "Small chance of that! I phoned her from San Juan. She's still with her sister in Sydney and with a little luck she'll like it so much she'll stay there. It was worth taking the risk, wasn't it?"

She looked at him from under half-lowered eyelids, unconsciously everting her lips. "You know it was," she said. "The waiting gets on my nerves at times, that's all it is. Don't pay any attention to my moods."

* * *

Jenny's replacement was waiting at the quayside when the ship docked again in Florida, a cocky Australian with tanned skin and white hair. She could imagine him being a tiger among the cabin stewardesses. Before she left, the purser handed her a cheque for a highly satisfactory sum – more than satisfactory until she realised that it was in dollars. Even Jonas Briggs said that it had been good working with her. He presented her with a bottle of duty-free perfume as a going-away present and kissed her cheek, leaving behind a taint of duty-free whisky.

She suffered again the indignity and squalor of the 767. When Jenny got home she found a print of the couple among her personal photographs. She meant to send it to him but only then realised that he had avoided telling her his name.

* * *

Jenny returned home to a flurry of activity. Belated Christmas presents were exchanged. She had carried out her Christmas shopping in such exotic locations as Martinique and San Juan, where a strong pound, an absence of duty and a readiness to haggle had produced a purchasing power which stretched the remains of her money far beyond where it would have reached at home. Her friends and family were properly impressed. They, for their part, had chosen for her some suitably priced items from a long list of photographic goods which she had said were absolute necessities.

She paid off the balance on the scooter with her earnings from the cruise ship and had enough left over for another camera body in time for the start of the new term. Until Dan Mandible sold a shot of a family stranded on the roof of their car after a nearby river burst its banks in the February floods, she was penniless again.

After being accepted as a professional in the sunshine, it was a shock to the system to return to a British winter and to being a student again, lectured and harassed and intimidated with threats of failure. The musty smell of the Tech corridors and classrooms was a poor exchange for the trade winds and the scent of flowers. But Jenny was determined, and young enough to be resilient.

For a few minutes, when a trio of fire appliances overtook her – once again while she was returning home from an evening class – she thought that the gods might be smiling on her. She twisted open the throttle of the scooter and pursued them, skidding slightly on the greasy tarmac, to the outskirts of the city where the premises of a paint and varnish wholesaler were well alight. Two more appliances arrived from the opposite direction to help deal with the mounting blaze. She found, however, that she had been beaten to the punch. An obvious professional was already at work. She took a few shots of the fire and of the gathering crowd, avid for the drama of the flames which were roaring skyward and painting their faces with hellish light. Her zoom lens enabled her to take the shots from just far enough away that the flash still left the flame-light dominant. These might be for her own collection and the end-of-course exhibition. Or, she hoped, Dan might be able to find somebody who would buy them – perhaps to illustrate a book about abnormal psychology, she thought wryly.

A sudden onset of diffidence might have prevented her from approaching the professional, but he was using the latest digital camera, to which they had just been introduced at the Tech. Dan Mandible had been advising her to invest in the recent technology on the grounds that the resultant shots could be fed direct into a computer or sent over the phone without the intermediate degradation usually inflicted by a scanner. She had retorted that he would have to sell whole albums of her photographs before she could afford such luxuries.

All the same, she had been bitten by the acquisitive bug.

The fire was still at its height but the other photographer, his needs presumably satisfied, was packing up and heading for a small but businesslike Ford which had been parked on the other side of the road. She caught up with him as he put a key in the lock.

She had been turning over possible approaches in her mind, but she heard herself asking bluntly, "What paper are you from?"

He looked at her in surprise for a moment. He was an elderly man. His clothes, his face, even his car, everything about him except his camera had a worn-out look. "The *Tidings*," he said. "Why?"

"Are you Charlie?"

His eyebrows arched even higher. "That's right. Night duty photographer."

"I brought in the shots of the Westerlink fire. You said they were very good, all things considered."

His shy smile took about fifteen years off his apparent age. "I meant it," he said. "You must be Jenny Ambleton. I've been seeing your photo-credit here and there."

"I'm doing the course in photography at the Tech. I wanted to ask you about the pros and cons of a digital camera like that one."

He glanced at his watch. "I've got all I need. Let me drop this in to the office and I'll sneak out and buy you a drink. That's the first advantage of the digital – you don't have to hang around processing films."

"You're on," she said. "That's the best offer I've had in the last ten minutes."

"Pull into the staff car park behind the *Tidings* building."

Jenny had ignored such trivia as speed limits on the way to the fire but she obeyed them strictly on the way back. Charlie, it seemed, had no such inhibitions, relying on his employers to reimburse him for any fines. He vanished down the road with a whirr and a clatter and was emerging from the building into the car park as she stopped the scooter and pulled it up onto its stand.

"I'd better phone my parents. Is there— ?"

"Here," he said. "Use my mobile. The *Tidings* pays."

It felt strange to be speaking to her father from a street corner. She decided that she must, really must, lash out for a mobile phone one of these days. She returned the phone and hung the strap of her camera bag over her shoulder. It was becoming heavier by the day but it was too valuable to be left on the scooter.

The pub was poky and unpretentious but it was warm and welcoming, with a babble of cheerful voices, many of them *Tidings* staffers knocking off in succession as the paper made its gradual progress towards publication. Charlie ignored several ribald shafts of wit and led Jenny to a table near the fire. She was dressed for the cold night and the scooter and she began to roast. She removed her anorak and a cardigan. Somebody began to hum the opening bars of 'The Stripper'.

"Pay no attention. What'll you take? Gin and tonic?" he asked her.

"Thank you kindly and don't ever stop asking me, but I've got to ride home," she said. "Half-pint shandy will do. And I should be buying the drinks. I want to pick your brains."

"Pick away, but no girl student buys my drinks. I'm old-fashioned that way and I know what student finances are like." He went to the bar, returning with her shandy and what looked like a large whisky for himself. He saw her eyes on his glass. "It's all right for me," he said. "I live nearby. I don't have to worry about driving home and it's handy if the Prime Minster spontaneously combusts on the Town Hall steps in the small hours."

"Does he often do that?"

"No, but he should. I live in hope."

They settled down. She was at ease with him, perhaps due to their common bond in photography, and she was happy to find someone whose levity of speech matched her own. He spoke for a while about the electronic digital camera, comparing convenience with quality. On the comparative costs he was vague, having become used to an employer who provided his tools and materials. But, "Wait before you buy," he told her. "The costs are coming down by the minute."

When that topic seemed to be exhausted, he said, "You really want to become a freelance?"

"I think so. Unless I can find a job that pays good money for no effort but lots of talent."

Charlie nodded. "Somebody put an ad in the *Tidings* once. It said 'Servile creep seeks lucrative sinecure.' When you come to think about it, that says it all. It describes what both parties are looking for. There was a box number and the girl told me that several replies came in. I often wonder how he got on." Charlie fell silent for a moment, still wondering. "My job will come vacant soon, when I retire. But if you're good – and you will be – you'd be better off as a freelance. In my old age, I enjoy the easy life. The money comes in once a month whether I succeed or fail. I'm finished by sparrow-fart, sleep until noon and have the best part of the day to myself. Shall I hand out some more advice?"

"Yes, please. I collect advice. Some day I'll put it all in a book. I'll change my name to Jenny Stone and I'll call it *Tablets of Stone.*"

"This bit is not for publication. It's no skin off my nose," he said earnestly, "if you scoop the rest of the world. But I don't want you scooping me. Anything you get by doing what I'm about to tell you, you check with me before offering it to the *Tidings*. Fair enough?"

"Perfectly," she said.

Charlie glanced round the bar and lowered his voice. "Newspapers usually have informants in the emergency services who give them a tip-off when something news-worthy comes up. You can't compete with that but, of course, a policeman or a fireman can't always dash to the phone while there's an emergency on. We don't always get the tips in time to take photographs. So get yourself a radio, a portable, a good one which includes UHF and VHF as well as the waveband between a thousand and fifteen hundred metres. That's between medium and long wave. Those are where nearly all the fire, police and ambulance radio traffic is. If you monitor those wavebands, you'll hear most of what's going on. A lot of the police traffic is encrypted so you'll lose that, but you'll get the rest. The only reason you beat me to the Westerlink fire was that I was listening to an ambulance being directed to an accident. By the time it turned out to be a false alarm – the woman had fallen off a chair while hanging curtains – the fire was out."

Jenny was intrigued but also cautious. "Isn't it illegal to listen in?"

"Having the set isn't illegal. They get a bit uptight about people listening in to their radio traffic, but they don't usually know. Just don't make the mistake of arriving at the scene before they do and whenever you get out of the car leave the set tuned to your favourite pop station."

"I see that I'll have to start saving up all over again," she said ruefully.

He laughed the youthful laugh which came so oddly from his aged face. "It may not be as bad as that. Just sell a few shots. The *Tidings* is looking for some good space-fillers for Mondays. Nothing much happens at weekends and nobody likes working on a Sunday, so Monday's paper is sometimes hard to fill. Would you mind being called out at night if I'm not available or when two incidents happen at the same time?"

"Not very much," she said.

"Leave your phone number with me and I'll see that the desk has it available."

"God bless you, my noble benefactor," Jenny said. "When I'm rich, I'll buy you a drink in return."

Three

The year began the long climb up towards spring. Jenny would have thought that Charlie had forgotten his promise of work, except that she had two call-outs, one to a spectacular late evening fire at a paper works while Charlie was at the airport and awaiting the crashing of a plane with undercarriage failure (which disappointed the waiting media by making it safely onto the ground), the other to an unimportant mayoral function while Charlie had the 'flu.

There was also a call-out to what proved to be a false alarm and Jenny was both pleased and surprised to be paid for one of her favourite occupations, riding the empty streets at night. She began to forgive the *Tidings* for its earlier treatment of her. There was no doubt, however, that the weight of her camera bag was becoming enough seriously to unbalance the scooter and the jaunt would have been safer and more comfortable if made on four wheels rather than two. She took her driving lessons very seriously, asking her instructor many questions (some of which he was hard put to it to answer) and getting practice on the family's cars whenever the various owners would permit.

Aided by the three commissions plus some shots of a

lorry crushed by a fallen tree, Jenny did manage to buy the radio, a model recommended by her friend Charlie; but she was making little progress towards other planned extravagances and, with her course accelerating in content, she had little time for cruising around on spec.

She was also finding home life a little restrictive. Her course required a grounding in traditional techniques and this necessitated a considerable amount of darkroom work. The darkrooms at the Tech were few, overused and usually left in a mess by the previous user and the equipment was often unserviceable. Jenny was meticulously tidy in her work and preferred to take her time over it. An importunate banging on the darkroom door by the next comer she found singularly off-putting and the vibration could soften the sharpness of any enlargements in train. When possible, she avoided their use.

A small and cheap enlarger, capable of producing good enlargements when allied to one of her camera lenses, had been among the acquisitions after her service on the cruise ship, but she had no darkroom of her own. The family kitchen was uncurtained and brightly lit by a street lamp outside and her use of the only bathroom had to be restricted to a time after the family had gone to bed. Even so, a whole spool of film from the portraiture class was ruined when her father felt a sudden call of nature in the night. If only she could afford a place of her own.

The opportunity was to come sooner than she expected. In the middle of March, her radio warned her of an impending strike by firemen at the airport. Jenny was stale with studying. She knew that lack of firemen brought take-offs and landings to a halt, so she set off for the airport. There was little hope of high drama but scenes of stranded passengers and idle planes might sell.

As she neared the airport car parks, she noticed a large black limousine parked, almost lurking, in an inconspicuous corner behind a filling station. This, she had noticed in the past, meant that somebody important, or somebody who considered himself important or wanted to be thought so, was attempting or pretending to arrive incognito. She called in for a gallon of two-stroke and made a few tentative enquiries but the staff at the filling station denied that anyone was expected. All the same, when Jenny discovered that the threatened strike had been settled before it had begun, she decided to wait.

For nearly an hour, she darted to and fro through the milling herd of travellers, between lounges and gates, through queues and bars and restaurants, trying to cover the VIP lounge as well as every possible route through the terminal.

Had she already missed whoever-it-was? Heart in mouth, she made one dash outside and along the approach road. The stretched limousine was still where she had seen it. Should she stand guard there? But if it moved away suddenly she could never keep up with it on foot and by the time she could fetch the scooter her target might have come and gone. She scurried back to the terminal.

Eventually, a BA flight from the USA disgorged her quarry. She would have let the new arrivals go past unrecognised if her attention had not been caught by the entourage of minders and bag-carriers. When she looked again, a thousand bells began to ring. During the previous weeks it had been leaked to the media that a certain pop star had secretly married his childhood sweetheart

44

somewhere secret in southern California and the couple were rumoured to be honeymooning at an equally secret resort on some Pacific island. The story had meant little to her at the time because she disliked the pop star and considered his performance to be no more than a tuneless whine and his music second rate and largely plagiarised, but he had a huge following among the teenyboppers and the story had had more than its fair share of coverage, all the more because no pictures had been released. The tongues of the media were hanging out worldwide for photographs. It came back to her now that, according to the *Tidings*, the pop star and his bride had both originated in the city and there had been speculation as to whether they would return so that each could meet the other's family or whether the families would be flown out to join them on his ranch near Las Vegas.

She had spotted them on the tarmac from the observation gallery, but they vanished from sight somewhere below her feet before coming within camera range in the uncertain light. Jenny's guess was that they would be spirited through the VIP lounge and out through some side door.

Jenny was becoming wise to the tricks used by and against the Press. She raced down to the main entrance doors and looked around. Daylight had faded and the street lights were making reflections on the tarmac. The limousine was on the move towards a corner of the terminal. Jenny sprinted after it, fumbling in her bag as she went for her camera, to which she had already attached the flash unit.

As she skidded round the corner, almost pulled off her feet by the weight of her bag, the happy couple, still surrounded by their entourage, emerged from an inconspicuous door no more than ten yards away from her and started the few paces to the car. They were obviously grubby and exhausted from travelling but they were indisputably and recognisably there. Jenny slithered to an abrupt halt. She just had time to check the focus and make sure that the settings were near enough. She took one photograph. The light was poor, the flash was necessary and it would take seconds for the battery to recharge the capacitor. There would be no second chances.

At the flash, the whole party hesitated. A large man, evidently a bodyguard, lunged at her. "Here," he said. "Give me that."

Jenny thrust the camera under her anorak, which seemed to nonplus the man. His instructions with regard to laying hands on young women must have been unclear. "No, please," Jenny said to the singer in what she hoped was a suitably whining voice. "It's only for my young sister. She thinks you're fabulous." She wanted to add ". . . and so do I," but the words stuck in her throat.

"Oh, leave her, Bert," said the pop star wearily. "It's bound to happen some time." Lacking the familiar microphone, he had to raise his voice until it cracked, to be heard above the roar of a plane lifting off. The couple and half their companions entered the stretched limousine and were wafted away. Moments later, a second car pulled in and gathered up the others and Jenny found herself alone on a corner of pavement, wondering if it had all really happened. (One advantage of a digital camera, she told herself, was that she could have reviewed the shot via the viewfinder for reassurance.)

But this was no time for wondering and doubt. She

dashed back into the terminal and searched for an idle telephone.

For two days, the newlyweds were holed up in the principal suite of the city's best hotel while members of their families were escorted in to visit them and the world's press laid unsuccessful siege. Jenny's one photograph was all that was available and Dan sold it worldwide while Jenny wondered why on earth anybody would pay good money for a poor photograph of a talentless vocalist and his pug-faced bride. Then the first marital disagreement exploded into a storm and the bride, less than half dressed, ran out of the suite in tears with the groom in hot pursuit, all under the eyes and lenses of the press. Jenny's photograph became, literally, yesterday's news. But it had had its day and a day is a long time in the media world.

* * *

Dan Mandible's cheque arrived while Jenny was preparing for what would be the final written exams. The sum seemed monstrous, quite out of proportion for such a brief moment of work and even more so when she realised that it really was in pounds this time, but she had little leisure to gloat over it. She deposited the cheque with the bank, took a small sum for day-to-day expenses, and returned to her studies. After the written exams, there was material to prepare for the final exhibition of student work on which they would be judged. The course led to no more than a certificate which might be of use when applying for a low-key job, nothing more, but despite her sometimes flippant manner everything that she did Jenny took seriously. She worked mostly at home.

She was working on the dining-room table, cropping the penultimate enlargement of the set architectural subject, a Norman church with elaborate vaulting and Jacobean woodwork, when her mother called her to the phone. Reluctantly, she tore herself away from making the most of a sharply illuminated and heavily carved Norman chancel arch.

"You owe me two hundred quid," said a voice.

"In a pig's ear," Jenny said. She was in no mood to be interrupted by chancers who had heard of her lucky break. "Who is this?"

"Jonas. Jonas Briggs. Remember me?"

"Yes, of course I do, Jonas," Jenny said penitently. "What's the matter? Did the purser get our payments cocked up?"

"Nothing like that. The old boat's gone in for her refit and I got the chance to buy the equipment real cheap, because it's a bit dated. It's still good, though. The developer, the printer and the odds and sods. Do you want it or are you leaving me stuck with it?"

Jenny had asked about the equipment on the spur of the moment while vaguely envisaging a future which included processing films for herself and others. She had since found that a processing laboratory less than a mile away could do most of the work better and cheaper than the comparative amateur in the family bathroom, but when it came to producing enlargements of selected portions of a colour negative and other more ambitious work there was no substitute for the personal attention of the photographer. The process of colour printing was infuriatingly temperature-sensitive and the proper machine would make all the difference. Moreover, the processing lab did not have a seven-day, twenty-four-hour service. Dan had emphasised more than once that he could obtain better terms when he had the photographs in his hand rather than undeveloped film and that those terms were highest for the first hour or two, before the other vultures caught up. And anyway, she could hardly leave Jonas Briggs who, for all the surly face that he presented to the world, had proved to have a heart of gold, in his own words 'stuck with it'.

"I'll take it," she said. "I only wish I'd had it for the past fortnight. Where is it now?"

"In my son's garage. It's taken me days to find the beer mat I wrote your phone number on. Guess where it was."

"Under a mug of beer?"

"Right."

"Can you hang on to it for a few more days?" Jenny asked. "I'm doing my finals."

"No problem."

Jenny was surprised to find that her material in the students' exhibition took up twice the space of anyone else's and that most of the others' work was of the College's set-pieces plus a few shots of buildings and scenery. As soon as the exhibition had been seen by the examiners, interested members of the public (principally the friends and family of the students) were given a day to view it. The students were then free to reclaim their own work – all but those items particularly favoured by the College, which had retained the right to hold them for a year as testament to the teaching ability of the staff. Jenny was flattered to find that several of her own photographs had been taken down, including a shot of rapt and dramatically lit faces at the paint depot fire.

Jenny was free at last to graduate from apprenticeship to real life. A huge void was opening in front of her through which she could travel as she wished. But her first steps were already clear in her mind. She prevailed on her brother to borrow a van from a friend and the two made a round trip of a hundred miles each way. Jenny found herself the possessor of a type LR Konika developing machine, a Durst printer and the accompanying Propax print developer. To her surprise, Jonas had also produced a receipt from the shipping line for exactly the amount quoted. She had been sure that he had added on a commission for himself.

It was the turn of Jenny's father's garage to house the substantial pieces of equipment and he made it known that he was none too happy about an arrangement that resulted in his car having to stand outside. True, it was summer and fine weather had arrived at last, but there had been visits from joyriders in the neighbourhood. A neighbour's newly acquired and much prized car had been driven away and torched.

It seemed to Jenny that the time for fleeing the nest had arrived.

At last she had the time and the spare mental capacity to consider the windfall which had followed the short-lived marriage of the pop star. When she looked at her bank statement the balance to her credit seemed enormous beyond the dreams of avarice, but when she compared it with house prices the sum was not so astronomic after all. "It would have been much larger," Dan Mandible said, "if the little bastards had managed to rub along together for another week." Jenny retorted that it would also have been larger if he hadn't taken fifteen per cent of it. But it was still a very useful sum and she admitted to herself that, without his marketing skills, she would probably have settled for a third of the amount.

Her parents, while delighted at her good fortune, had been assuming that the money would be left to grow as protection against the proverbial rainy day. Mr Ambleton had been lavish with his advice about safe investments with capital appreciation. But Jenny was embarking on Life. Numbers on paper would not give her mobility nor keep the rain off. Now was the time to spend. Old age could look after itself for the moment.

She had had the foresight to apply for a driving test some weeks earlier. The day arriving, her facility with mechanical things came to her aid and she passed at the first try. Without even returning home, she persuaded her instructor to let her drive to where she had seen what she considered to be suitable vehicles for sale and when she arrived home it was in a small Japanese-made jeep. This had the singular advantages that it could go almost anywhere and that the front part of the roof could be slid back, allowing her to stand on the front seats for the higher viewpoint that she often needed. No more balancing on skips for Jenny.

Even more adventurous steps were to follow. A day spent studying the affordable end of the market soon convinced her that there was nothing to be rented which she would care to occupy, especially when it entailed seeing a substantial sum vanish every month, never to return, and that houses, at least respectable houses, were beyond her means unless she obtained a mortgage. She had no intention of setting out to earn a living with the proverbial millstone round her neck.

But there were flats for sale within her budget figure. One of these was almost opposite the fire station. It had been on the market for some months, presumably because potential buyers did not fancy being woken in the night whenever some fool set his chimney on fire. But to Jenny, this was no disadvantage. She had come to regard fires as terribly bad luck for somebody, usually an insurance company, but they had brought her nothing but money. It was a classic case of meat and poison and an ill wind blowing some good in her direction. Firelight was her lucky star. The flat was on the ground floor of a small block of flats, recently built by the council on a gap site in a broad tree-lined street. The flats had later been sold off to sitting tenants, one of whom was now cashing his investment. Street parking was available at the front and there was a small private car park at the back of the building.

The flat was empty and unencumbered. The seller was delighted to accept slightly less than the asking price from a young lady with immediate cash and no other property to sell. A surveyor gave the flat his blessing and the deeds were signed and the keys delivered in a matter of days.

Then, and only then, Jenny told her parents.

Their reaction was remarkably moderate. After they had had their say on such subjects as extravagance and secretiveness, her father uttered dire warnings about financial disaster and predatory men and her mother suddenly felt old and useless and was sure that Jenny would soon starve to death; but in his heart of hearts Mr Ambleton was relieved to get his garage back and to have one less mouth to feed so much earlier than he had expected, while his wife accepted that, if Jenny had come to the age for frolicking with young men, she would prefer to know as little as possible about it.

The flat comprised a sitting room and kitchen separated by a dining recess, a bathroom far too small for her photographic purposes and two bedrooms. A second-hand kitchen fitment, advertised in the *Tidings* and bought for a song, would go a long way towards converting the smaller bedroom into a passable darkroom. The existing decorations were acceptable if totally unimaginative; limitations of time and money dictated that they would have to suffice for the foreseeable future.

For the rest, the Ambletons decided that the time had come to replace some furniture. Jenny would be allowed to take her own bed, the living-room suite and a very much scratched-up table which would be immediately consigned to the new darkroom.

After much heart-searching, Jenny had invested in the recommended digital camera, the computer which would process its productions and hold the index on which Dan Mandible was still insisting and also a good printer. Her once healthy bank account was now suffering something akin to battle-fatigue, but at least during her remaining days at home she could inveigle her mother, who had an aptitude for computers unusual in her generation, to make a start at computerising the index of negatives, which had so far existed only as scribbles on old pieces of wrapping paper.

She continued to sleep at her old home while waiting for a local plumber and electrician to connect the sink and add electric points to the darkroom and elsewhere. During the days that this took, she visited the flat daily, partly in the hope of accelerating the work, partly to transport piecemeal some books and chattels in her jeep and partly, she admitted secretly, in the hope of meeting and impressing the young man with the resonant voice who seemed to live across the hall. She had met him once in the outside doorway and he had seemed to have all the qualities of Jenny's ideal. He was tall. A crooked nose suggested an interest in masculine sports. He was freshly shaven and smelled faintly of aftershave. His shoes were good and freshly polished but in all other respects his clothes were casual and practical. (Jenny, whose dress sense leaned heavily towards jeans, sweaters and loose anoraks, was sure that, in this respect at least, they must be twin souls.) He had carried indoors, with no apparent effort, a box of books which had tested her strength to the utmost. At the time, he had spoken no more than a few polite words of enquiry as to when she would be moving in, but Jenny was sensitive to voices and his almost musical tones sent shivers up her spine.

Meanwhile, money had to be earned to pay the bills. She had thought of advertising for portrait work, weddings and christenings, and of putting herself into the Yellow Pages but had been warned not to invite increased local taxes nor to fall foul of the dreaded Change of Use. She would have to survive on what she and Dan Mandible could generate between them.

Dan had followed up the hint given to Jenny by her friend Charlie and had at last finalised a deal with the *Tidings* picture editor. A space would be held for Jenny in every Monday's copy, which was to be filled by something local, interesting, topical, beautiful and either funny or a tear-jerker, under the heading 'SEEN RECENTLY' and her photo credit. As long as she managed to satisfy those conditions and the feature remained popular, the arrangement would continue on quite favourable terms. If not, the paper reserved the right to terminate.

Many of Jenny's negatives most suited to use as amusing space-fillers were of obviously winter scenes which could hardly be passed off as high summer, but might serve to plug a gap later. The first Monday was to be catered for by an incident which she had captured in the first heat of enthusiasm a year earlier. This had been at the beach where a fat lady was attempting the universal trick of dressing under a towel, but hampered and embarrassed by the sudden arrival of a strong wind. After that, new material would be urgently needed. (The lady later threatened to sue until it was pointed out to her that she was unlikely to be recognised from the photograph, whereas any move towards litigation would reveal her identity to the whole world.)

Although she had chosen that flat in preference to others on offer partly because from it she would be able to hear the sound of fire appliances going out (in the hope that fires, if they had to happen, might continue to be lucky for her), Jenny's next fire, and one of the most significant, occurred before she had even moved into the flat.

That day Jenny set off in her jeep, following the routes which, in the past, had been most productive of material for her lenses. A thin veil of high cloud was diffusing the sunlight perfectly for photography but either the humans and animals of the city were behaving in a manner less eccentric or less photogenic than previously or Jenny, now that her livelihood depended on it, was more critical of the material to be encountered. Whatever the reason, it seemed that her luck was out. She circled the shopping districts (a mixture of old buildings with shops tucked in at street level and long modern complexes with parking tucked in above and below), she looped round by the docklands (cobbled and smelling of fish and diesel) and visited the beaches, all to no good effect. As the shadows lengthened, she decided to visit the park in the hope that the evening light would lend the familiar scene some extra pictorial value.

The new radio was muttering away by her side and periodically she toyed with the 'Search' control. As she neared the park, this homed in on a Fire Service call, diverting an appliance from a cat in a tree to back two others which were speeding to a house fire. Charlie had explained to her that a single fire appliance might be responding to a chimney fire or a boy with his head stuck in the railings, but three or more would certainly be for something serious. Jenny would have preferred the boy and the railings as being likely to amuse the reader without attracting rival photographers, but she decided to follow it up. The quoted address was not far away.

She swooped round three corners and checked. Her mental map of the prosperous suburb was at fault. She parked and stopped her engine and listened. She could hear the klaxon of a fire appliance somewhere to her right. She took the next turning in that direction and saw the fire scene ahead, almost dead-heating with the last of the fire engines. The street, for most of its length, was so orderly that a badly parked car or an overgrown lawn would have been cause for head-shaking, but one stretch broke the pattern. Fire appliances and scattered pedestrians milled around an otherwise typical house of, Jenny guessed, around six bedrooms and almost as many baths. This was upmarket territory.

Behind the downstairs windows, the flickering yellow light of flames came and went behind a shroud of smoke. Upstairs, there seemed to be more smoke than anything else but, with the dread instinct that alerts ghouls to disaster, a small crowd was already gathered, watching the few good neighbours who had been trying ineffectually to do something useful. Jenny parked at a suitable vantage point, protruded herself from the waist up through the open roof of the jeep and photographed the bystanders with the digital camera. But she was not yet familiar enough with its use to be confident of good results, so she dropped it back into its nest in her new camera case, closed the roof and got out with her faithful Pentax, locking the jeep carefully behind her. There was too much money tied up in that camera case for her to take chances with its contents.

The substantial two-storey house dated from early in the 1900s and seemed to have been very well kept. The garden, now suffering from the activities of the firefighters, had once been as immaculate as its neighbours. Smoke was leaking from the few ventilators and all the windows now had a grey haze resembling eyes with cataracts. Jenny waited, taking more shots of the growing crowd. The fire itself would be more spectacular in its later stages. The firemen had found the doors locked and one of them was running towards the solid-looking front door with an axe.

There was a communal gasp from the watchers, like a sigh from the angel of death. Jenny followed the direction of the many eyes and felt a sudden prickling of the skin over her whole body. A face had appeared at an upper window. It was a woman, Jenny was sure; a woman with her dark hair adrift. She seemed to move sluggishly and yet panic showed in every movement. Her mouth was open and she seemed to be calling out, but the rest of her face was distorted by fear. She was wrestling with the window catches while her whole body shook with coughing. Jenny wanted to rush to her aid but she knew that there was nothing that she could do except get in the way of the firefighters.

The front door gave and firemen masked with breathing equipment moved in. Flames flared out of the door. At the same time, a ladder was being readied. Somebody shouted to the woman that help was on the way although the shout could not have been heard through the glass. She had given up her struggle with the window catches and had begun attacking the glass with a shoe. Now she came at it with a chair. Jenny realised that the old glass had been replaced with modern double glazing, very difficult to break. But at the third attempt she drove a hole through a large pane.

Immediately, as the fumes received a supply of oxygen, there was a flashover. Flame roared through the room and flowered through the broken window. The woman vanished but for another few seconds they could hear her screams. Then she was mercifully silent.

Four

L ooking back later, it seemed to Jenny that the scene had, until that moment, been muted, almost silent. The noise of the flames was held within the building, the onlookers seemed dumbstruck and the firefighters went about their business with unspeaking efficiency. Even the engines of the appliances seemed muffled. Suddenly, the scene flared into noise – the screams of the woman, suddenly cut off; the roar of flames; the shocked babble of the onlookers and the hiss of hoses. All the windows were now back-lit with glare. Soon, smoke was leaking between the roof tiles. The house, within its outer shell, was largely built of timber and had been dried by central heating for most of a century. The fire took hold with awesome rapidity. The firemen were driven out and could only use their hoses to pour water onto the roof and through broken windows.

Jenny was helpless. Her mouth was dry and her limbs were shaking. The woman had died before her eyes, gone to her maker, terminated. To the old, death may approach as a friend, but to the young it is fearsome beyond all else. Jenny found that she was crying. There was nothing else that she could do except follow her calling and record the scene. The woman, surely, was already beyond pain. Word circulating among the watchers was that the stairs had already been too far gone to be climbed – Jenny absorbed this information in the half-intuitive way that word passes among crowds. It seemed that her hands had been working away throughout, unprompted except by habit.

She was mercifully distracted from thoughts of death by the sudden recognition of a perfect picture. In the hedge where she stood, a blackbird was brooding her chicks, refusing to quit her nest but keeping an anxious eye on the flames. It was a perfect commentary, an encapsulation of the whole lottery of life – death and renewal, with some creatures surviving but most falling by the wayside. The roof fell in with a blaze of flame and sparks. Jenny concentrated on capturing the bitter-sweet scene, the mother hen with her nest intact, silhouetted against the out-of-focus burning house. She braced herself with care because her hands were still unsteady. As she did so, she wondered at herself. Was she being unfeeling? Or was she learning the dissociation of mind from emotion that the good reporter needs? There would be time enough, she hoped, for introspection later.

She had just released the shutter when a voice spoke behind her. "I *said* that we'd have to catch the bugger before he killed somebody." The tone was distraught, the accent nearly but not quite Oxford and the voice itself could have been that of an operatic baritone.

Jenny span round. Her neighbour was looking past her shoulder at the pyre. His face was grim. He glanced at her and recognised her surprise. "I'm sorry," he said quickly. "Did I speak aloud? I didn't mean to. You saw the woman?"

"I saw. It was terrible," Jenny said. Her voice, like his, was not quite steady. "Not to be able to do anything . . . Did you mean that somebody set the house on fire deliberately?"

The young man seemed confused. "We won't know that until it cools down and the fire investigators can move in. I spoke without thinking. Please forget what I said. I was probably talking nonsense."

Forgetting would have been impossible. "But who are you?" she asked. "What are you? Who's 'we'? You may as well tell me. I live just across the hall from you, so I'm bound to find out some time."

He looked at her, seeing her for the first time. "I helped you carry a box of books," he said. "That was you? You look different."

Jenny refused to feel insulted. "I look cleaner and tidier. Not much but a little. Removals are a messy business. Your turn. What are you?"

He hesitated and then shrugged. "I'm a police officer. But I'd rather that you didn't shout it from the rooftops. Usually, either the neighbours turn hostile or they expect you to keep the whole neighbourhood quiet and law-abiding in your spare time."

"I won't tell anybody." They fell silent. Apart from his voice there was little, she thought, to distinguish him. He was of average height and average build, but apparently well muscled and athletic. He had brown hair with only a slight wave to it, eyes of no particular colour and a face which might have been passably good-looking before his nose was trodden on.

61

His front teeth were a little too straight and white to be natural. He was wearing a T-shirt printed with a picture of a full-rigged clipper, tracksuit trousers and trainers.

The fire was at its height now. Beside the three fire appliances, an ambulance was standing by.

The silence between them had gone on for too long. She had promised not to reveal his occupation but she had said nothing about his incautious words. She wanted to change the subject, quickly before he thought to extract another promise from her, but no other subject came to her mind. She was almost relieved when a ululating shriek broke up the tête-à-tête.

Even the firefighters seemed to pause in their work. Jenny span round, her heart jumping. She knew that her jeep was fitted with an alarm but she had never heard it in action. The youth who had been trying to open the lock was at least as startled as she was, but after a moment of stunned inaction he took to his heels and ran, vanishing between the houses before Jenny, hampered by the need to preserve the camera bouncing on her chest, could cross the street.

Bemused by so many dramatic events in succession, Jenny fought to remember the salesman's instructions on how to silence the alarm. She managed at the second attempt and relocked the jeep. When she returned across the street, her neighbour was still there. "Any damage?" he asked.

"Just superficial," she said. "Should I report it?"

"I wouldn't bother. There's nothing that anybody can do about it now. It's not as if he'd taken anything that might be recovered."

"For a policeman," she said, half joking, "you weren't a lot of help."

He nodded seriously. "I'm a detective. I mustn't leave a scene to chase a petty criminal. You were doing fine on your own. If he'd turned on you, I'd have been there in two jumps. Excuse me. The fire officers may have time to talk to me now, before the really messy bit begins."

He moved away. Jenny took two more shots of the nest, but the light was fading and the fire was coming under control. Just as the hoses subdued the last of the flames, Charlie's tired old car arrived and the *Tidings* photographer hurried to join her.

"Too late, am I? I was covering a mayoral press conference about absolutely nothing that anyone could possibly want to know and nobody called me. What happened?"

"House fire," Jenny said tersely. "Loss of life and I think there's some suspicion that an arsonist's working locally, but don't quote me personally on that."

"You caught it all?"

"All of it. Even the woman's face in the window. Not that I suppose you'll publish that. Too harrowing for friends and relations."

"That's up to the editor. Take your film out. We'll buy it off you."

"I've heard that one before," Jenny said. "I got a handful of peanuts and your bosses sold my shots all over the world. No, thank you very much. You're going to buy the shots one by one through my agent or not at all. He may be able to sell the gruesome ones to some Continental tabloid. Have you got your mobile phone on you?"

Charlie surrendered his phone after only a token protest. Jenny called Dan Mandible's number and Dan answered. Jenny gave him the bare facts, suppressing her own emotional reactions. She kept telling herself to remain detached. She held the phone so that Charlie could hear Dan's voice.

"Stay where you are," Dan said. "I'll be with you before you can scratch yourself. Fifteen minutes at the most."

"I'm a quicker scratcher than that," Jenny said. "I could meet you at the *Tidings* building, if you like. Charlie's wetting himself. He says nothing more's going to happen here until they bring the body out."

"He can't be sure of that. Let him bust a gut if he wants to. You wait for me."

"You heard the man," Jenny said. She began to wind back her film. "And, Charlie, if Dan lets you process it, be gentle with the negatives. Don't hurry them and end with grain like a gravel path, the way you would with any old shot to go with a story. There are some shots of a blackbird's nest against the flames that'll do well for my second featured spot."

"I'll be careful. Can I have my phone back now?"

"Certainly not. I haven't finished with it yet." Jenny removed the film, dropped it into her pocket under Charlie's covetous eyes and re-loaded the camera. Even in the wake of death, first things still came first. She always had spare films in her pocket, but an unloaded camera would be almost an invitation for the Martians to land. She used Charlie's phone to let her mother know that she would be late home. It was high time that she moved house, she thought, and a mobile phone had to rank high on her shopping list.

Charlie grabbed his phone back and shut himself in his car in order to ensure privacy while he called the night editor. When the few known facts had been transferred, together with the supposition of arson, he rejoined Jenny. "That'll set the wheels in motion," he said quietly. "Now all available staff will be phoning around, trying to get the police or the firemaster to confirm that there's a suspected arsonist at work."

"They won't confirm it, will they?"

"Not until they're good and ready. But a refusal to deny is almost as good."

"Your Mr Hines said something like that."

"I wonder who told him."

Dan Mandible arrived within his promised fifteen minutes, in a surprisingly sporty-looking saloon for one of his advanced age. He relieved Jenny of the film. "I'll go and talk to your night editor," he told Charlie.

"I'll meet you there," said Charlie. "Somebody will have to process the film." He gave Jenny back his mobile. "You stay here, Honeybunch, and catch the removal of the body. We'll buy that off you too. I'll call and tell you when tomorrow's edition goes to bed. After that, you'll know that there's no hurry."

Dan smiled grimly. "You may not be able to afford it," he said.

That reminded Jenny. It seemed callous to be talking money outside a house where somebody had just died, but she very much wanted to know. "How much are you going to ask?"

65

"I know how much I'm going to ask," Dan said, "but what I don't know is what I'll get."

"Put it another way," Jenny said. "Can I afford carpets for my flat?"

"I think I can promise you that much," Dan said, "provided that you stay away from antique Persian rugs. Now, I must dash!"

Jenny was left to her own devices. Now that the flames were dead and only the reek remained, the onlookers had nearly all dispersed to discuss the tragedy with bated breaths in the security of their own kitchens, only to be disturbed by police officers seeking information about who would have been in the house and the locations of any surviving kin. The questions were slanted tactfully in the direction of who had been seen in or around the house before the fire broke out.

Daylight faded but the scene remained brightly lit. One fire appliance still stood by in case of a rekindling, but the firemen could only wait, chatting with two uniformed constables. They looked as bored as Jenny felt. She stayed in the jeep, watching the passive scene under the floodlights and hoping for something to change. Life from now on, she supposed, would include long periods of waiting between bouts of hectic activity. Hadn't somebody once described war in similar terms? She wondered how she would react if a newspaper offered her a contract to go and cover a war. Refuse the job, probably, she decided, rather than go and disgrace herself.

She had the radio for company. She even continued to scan the emergency wavebands, but softly so as not to attract attention. While she waited, some other disaster might be occurring elsewhere.

A car, a top-of-the-range Audi, approached along the street, accelerated suddenly and then stopped with a yelp of tyres. Jenny, sensing a break in the long vigil, snatched up her camera and got out of the jeep. A man had sprung out of the Audi and grabbed one of the firemen by the sleeve. "What happened?" he demanded loudly. "How did it happen? *Is my wife all right?*"

As if by magic, some of the onlookers had reappeared.

The fire officer who appeared to be in charge hurried over. The man moved to meet him and so came into the glare of the floodlights. Jenny was surprised to recognise her acquaintance from the Westerlink fire and the cruise ship. Out of both delicacy and discretion, Jenny disconnected her flash unit before photographing the two men. The floodlights gave adequate illumination although the lamps nearest to the house had just been extinguished.

"Would your wife have been in the house?" the fire officer asked carefully.

"I suppose so. If she didn't go out. She . . . she had a migraine. She never goes out after a migraine. For God's sake, tell me what's happened."

The fire officer took a deep breath. "There's no easy way to say this, sir, but there seems to have been loss of life. A figure, apparently of a woman, was seen at an upstairs window. We don't know of any survivors. Would any other lady have been in the house?"

The man shook his head hopelessly and collapsed to sit on the low garden wall. He put his head down between his knees. Jenny's neighbour had joined the sad little group. "Detective Sergeant Welles," he said. "May I have your name?" There was no answer. He repeated the question.

The man raised his head slowly. His face seemed to be on the point of collapse. He hesitated as though he had difficulty recalling the answer. "Oliver," he said at last. "David Oliver."

One of the uniformed officers came between Jenny and the group. "You can't stay here, miss," he said. "We're taping the scene off to preserve evidence. Why don't you go home to bed?"

"I will," Jenny said. "Quite soon."

"I think you should go now. Is that your car over there?"

"The jeep? Yes."

"You'll have to remove it." Jenny must have looked rebellious. "May I see your driving licence?" he asked. She produced it. "And your MOT certificate? Insurance? And let's go and take a look at your tax disc, shall we, and measure the tread on your tyres?"

"All right," Jenny said wearily. "I get the message."

Almost opposite the burnt house a side street ran uphill. Jenny drove round a labyrinth of streets to return and find a place from which she could watch the front of the house a hundred yards away. So far, she had made little use of the big telephoto lens, but now she fitted it to the Pentax and found that what was left of the front door half-filled the frame. Mr Oliver was still in discussion with the fire officer and the policeman. His movements were agitated and at one point she thought that he was going to fall over. Her neighbour was writing steadily in a pocket book.

A woman's figure was waiting beside the hedge. When the other two men turned away, the woman moved forward and spoke to Mr Oliver. She led him to the house next door. He stumbled beside her as if he had lost his sight.

The floodlights nearest to the burnt house came on again – Jenny's guess was that some unusually sensitive officer had extinguished them during Mr Oliver's visit to spare him the sight of something that he might prefer not to see.

Charlie's mobile phone shrilled and she heard his voice announce that the paper had gone to bed.

She settled down to wait again, switching between channels to keep herself awake. The short hours of midsummer darkness soon passed and dawn came up. Still aware of the messages on the radio, she sank into a half-waking torpor through which were threaded dreams and daydreams that came and were as quickly forgotten. Repeatedly, the face at the window woke her with a jerk until she found herself fully awake and very cold. She knew that the embers had begun to cool when figures made bulky by protective clothing entered the empty shell and emerged again. The search for a body had begun.

The radio warned her when the body was about to be removed. She intercepted a radio message diverting an ambulance to the scene. Through the viewfinder and the telephoto lens she saw and photographed the body, decently shrouded, being brought out and loaded into the ambulance by figures in the same protective clothing. Stretching and yawning, she scribbled a note on a page from her notebook and drove round the silent streets to drop it, with the second film, through Dan Mandible's letterbox. Then she went home to bed.

Five

Sleeping until noon was not enough, but that day was the day she had appointed for the move to the new flat and her brother had borrowed the van again for that afternoon. She bolted a quick brunch while scanning the *Tidings*. Her pictures of the fire were prominently shown along with a photograph of the bereaved Mr Oliver in happier times but without, she noted, the face at the window. Mr Oliver, she saw, was said to be forty-six and the managing director of a large garden centre with an associated firm of landscaping contractors. On the same page but carefully separate from the news story was a headline, 'LOCAL ARSONIST AT WORK?' followed by a few paragraphs of rank speculation. Nobody from the police or the fire service had been available to comment. The editor had managed to invest the fact with significance.

Dan Mandible phoned before she had finished her meal. The *Tidings* had purchased the right to break the story, arson and all, but one or two of the nationals would have it for that evening's editions and one of the tabloids had bought the face at the window and was negotiating for the removal of the body. The photograph of Mr Oliver had been found in the *Tidings* library, but any shots of

71

the late Mrs Oliver – other than at the window during the last seconds of her life – now seemed to have been lost in the fire.

"I have one of the couple together," Jenny said. "They were on the cruise ship. I didn't realise whose house it was until he came home and got the news."

"Let's have it. All is grist, et cetera et cetera."

"Will a print do? I'm moving house this afternoon and I don't have time to look for negatives."

"I'll call at the flat later."

She had a few minutes in hand before the van would arrive and she used the time to phone a nearby furniture shop. She had already chosen her carpet and obtained a quote, without much hope of being able to afford such luxuries that year or possibly the next. Now she spoke to the carpet manager and told him to go ahead and lay the carpet – through all but the future darkroom, where bare flooring would have to suffice until she could afford tiles. "How soon can you do it?" she asked him.

"One moment." She heard the rustle of papers. "We have enough of it in stock and the fitters are quiet just now. Would tomorrow be soon enough?"

"If you can't manage anything sooner," Jenny said lightly. She disconnected and throttled back a yawn. She would sleep tonight if the face at the window did not come to haunt her. She would have dozed off if Dominic had not chosen that moment to arrive at the door.

Jenny's bed and the other furniture were loaded onto the van. With her father's help, the photographic machinery was put aboard. Vacant spaces were filled with some of her cartons, predominantly the lightweight ones which would be least trouble to move for the carpet fitters. She remembered belatedly and went back into the house, climbing into the attic to search another carton of half-forgotten odds and ends for the photograph.

It was a twenty-minute drive from the family home to her new abode; from placid suburbia to the bustling city. Dan Mandible was already waiting. He accepted the photograph but declined to help with the removal on ground of age and general feebleness.

"You just can't see a way to get fifteen per cent on it," Jenny said.

Dan was unruffled. "True. I'll see what I can do with the photograph," he said, "but the story may be past by tomorrow."

Jenny felt a momentary hollowness. She showed him the estimate for her carpets. "We should cover this all right," Dan said, "even if the story dies. If the arson story turns out to have foundation it may still not be more than a local story, but with loss of life . . . if nothing major breaks, everybody will want everything and they can have it . . . at a price."

"Drive a hard bargain. I need bed-linen and cutlery and crockery and furniture and . . . and . . ."

"And you shall have them, some day," Dan said. He smiled with his eyes and departed.

Jenny and her brother managed to wrestle everything into the flat, but at that point Dominic had to draw the line. He had been operating, he said, theoretically in his lunch-hour which had been over an hour ago and, anyway, Gus needed his van back. Jenny thanked her brother for his help, promised to do the same for him some day and allowed him to escape.

At least there was hot water in the taps and she had

brought soap and towels. She felt dusty and sticky and unfit for human company. Perhaps it would be a mistake, she admitted to herself, to shower and change before everything was in place but she felt unable to live with herself a minute longer. There was still work to be done if she were to sleep in her new home tonight and she was not at all sure that she could find any more clean clothes that she would be seen dead in. Perhaps if she took it easy and was careful not to get up a sweat . . . She treated herself to a shower and replaced her dirty clothes with a clean sweater and skirt from one of the cartons. Her mother would have dealt with the dirty clothes, returning them magically clean and fresh to her drawer, but she would have to manage without her mother now. And, she reminded herself, without drawers for the moment. Would it be in breach of her principles, she wondered, to visit home again with a bag of dirty laundry?

She had no more than a few minutes for contemplation before there was a tap on the front door, which opened directly from the hallway of the flats into her sitting room. She opened it to find the young man from across the hall (Detective Sergeant Welles, as she had now learned). "May I come in?" he asked formally.

"Do," she said. "If you can manage to ignore the mess." The shower and change of clothing no longer looked like a mistake, more a miracle of anticipation. "I can offer you a chair and nothing else. I'm still in the process of moving in."

"And looking as if you've done more than enough already," he retorted. "You take the chair and tell me where you want these things put."

She sank into the familiar comfort of one of the easy

chairs. "That's an offer I can't refuse," she said. "I should but I can't. The carpet fitters are coming in tomorrow, so if you could shift the cartons into the small bedroom, which is going to be my darkroom, you'd be a life-saver. I do feel as if I've lifted enough barges and toted enough bales for one day."

He grinned. "No problem," he said. He moved all the cartons.

"If I helped," she said, "do you think that we could move these machines? If not, I can probably sweet-talk the carpet fitters into doing it for me."

"Don't move," he said. "Let me feel the weight." He moved the photographic equipment single-handed where she and Dominic had had to struggle and then for an encore assembled her bed.

"And they say that our policemen are wonderful," she remarked.

"Who do?"

"I do. And our policemen say it all the time. I can't think of anyone else offhand. You've earned a cup of tea and I'd offer you one except that I still don't have a kettle. Or cups. Or tea, come to that. I was going to go across to the café, if you'd care to join me?" In an unaccustomed fit of shyness she felt that she was probably babbling.

But he was looking amused. "No need for that. I have all the makings and I came to have a word with you. Join me. You can return the invitation when you're more fully equipped."

"That may be some time off." She let him usher her into a mirror image of her own flat, furnished, to judge from the sitting room, robustly but with surprisingly good taste. The chairs were solid but comfortable – a man's choice. The bright wallpaper was well chosen if not always quite straight. "My parents," she said, "would give me half their chattels if I asked them, but they seem to think that I'm earning lots and lots of money and I'm in no hurry to disabuse them."

He said that he quite understood and for some reason she believed him. He left the room to put on the kettle, leaving her to look around. Among the few water-colours and the photographs of places and dogs, she spotted a group photograph of a rugby team. She picked out her host with some difficulty, which she realised was because his nose had not at that time been broken. She decided that his face had less in the way of good looks but much more character in its revised shape.

He returned with a tray bearing a teapot, a small biscuit tin, two mugs and a bottle half full of milk and set it down on the heaviest-looking pine coffee table that she had ever seen. If anybody was ever going to dance on a table in true night-club fashion, she decided, this should be the one.

"Not quite what you're used to at home," he said ruefully.

"But a lot more than what I've got." She guessed that he was not much in the habit of entertaining girls. For some reason, the thought pleased her.

He looked at his watch. "We have a few minutes in hand," he said. "So I'll tell you why I wanted to see you. By the way, did you feed the *Tidings* the rumour about the suspected arsonist?"

"You didn't exactly say not to," she retorted defensively. "And I didn't give you any promises, except about not telling the neighbours what you were."

He seemed surprised to get an honest admission instead of angry denial. "I believe that's right," he said after a moment's thought. "Next time I'll have to remember to get a promise from you. But there's no great harm done. My chiefs were on the point of holding a press conference anyway and enlisting the public's help."

"So there really is an arsonist?"

"We think so. Fire leaves very little evidence behind but there are usually pointers, and unless coincidence is at work we have the pointers here. You're Jenny Ambleton, aren't you?"

"I confess it," she said lightly, flattered that he had found out her name.

"I've seen photographs with your name attached. But you're not a newspaper employee?"

She shook her head. She was sorry now that she had recently had her hair bobbed. It flattered her features and moved attractively across her face – giving her, she thought, an air of mystery – but it also tended to blow in front of the lens. "I'm freelance," she said. "Trying to scratch a living out of whatever comes along."

"I can put some work your way. Nothing very remunerative," he added quickly, "but something to keep the pot boiling. Apropos which, I think this should be infused by now." He poured tea and offered her a digestive biscuit. Her mug came complete with a picture of the Simpsons. "But whatever I tell you now is confidential. Promise?"

"I promise."

He nodded. "It's this way. We're fairly sure that there's an arsonist at work – sure enough to have a team working on it. Not full-time – we have other cases – but steadily.

Because I was first on the scene of last night's fire I've been made responsible for liaison with the Fire Brigade and to act as SOCO – you know what that means?"

"Scene Of Crime Officer."

He nodded approvingly. "If, in fact, it turns out that there has been a crime. My own opinion so far, for what it's worth, is that it's a total waste of my time."

"Why do you think that? Or is it none of my business?"

"It doesn't seem to be part of the same series. The other suspicious fires were crude, petrol-and-a-match jobs. The university broke new ground with Fast Atom Bombardment Mass Spectrometry and something called –" he paused and took a deep breath "– Matrix-Assisted Laser Desorption Ionisation Time of Flight Mass Spectrometry, so that we know what brands of petrol were used. They even found tiny traces of rubber, probably from a siphoning tube. This was different. If it was started deliberately, which is by no means certain, it would have to have been something rather more sophisticated. It's too early to have hunches but I have one all the same. I think that this one may have been an accident. I'm meeting the Fire Investigating Officer and somebody from the Forensic Science Laboratory in –" he looked at his watch "– just over half an hour, by which time the ruin should be cool enough for proper investigation to begin. The snag is that we don't have a staff photographer available."

"Somebody was taking photographs last night. I saw the flashes."

"That was one of the firemen. But he's not a trained photographer, just a man with a Polaroid; and fire

78

officers are interested in what caused the fire whereas if a crime's been committed we're interested in evidence that will lead to a successful prosecution. A different wavelength altogether. But we have a problem. Between sickness, other cases and one honeymoon, we've run out of shutter-snappers for the moment, so I have authority to engage an outside professional. Do you know anything about fire scene photography?"

Jenny's course had included a lecture about preparing photographs for evidence and there had been a question in the final exam. "Record the number of the negative," she recited, "the date, time and location, the direction, the approximate subject, include a scale—"

"So you do know. Do you want to do it? There could be an advantage in using a photographer who was at the scene and saw the fire. Of course, I may be wasting your time as well as my own. On the other hand, I may not. The body's been removed – where it fetched up it could have been seen from the street – so you won't be required to inspect anything altogether too gruesome. There's a fixed rate of payment. Whether it's enough, I wouldn't know. The amount probably hasn't been revised since the days of Sir Robert Peel."

Jenny nearly said that she knew the body had been removed but decided that that would be lacking in discretion. "On the other hand," she said. "the costs of photography have come down a lot in real terms since the days of Sir Robert Peel. Glass-plate negatives used to cost the earth. Yes, of course I'll do it."

"Splendid! Drink your tea – no hurry – and we'll get out there. The fire officers can lend you some protective clothing. Bring several pairs of socks. Do you have everything else you'll need?"

"I've plenty of film. My only notebook's about the size of a postage stamp so I'll have to stop on the way to buy a proper one. Do you have one of those expanding metal tapes to use as a scale?"

"There's one in my car. And I can furnish a notebook."

"That's good. I'll bring my own pencil," she said.

He smiled suddenly. It lit up most of his face. Only his crooked nose remained neutral. "We might even be able to supply one of those," he said, "at the expense of the long-suffering taxpayer."

They sipped their tea. To break the silence, she said, "I was looking at your rugby team photograph. Is that how your nose got broken?"

His manner had been slightly stiff and avuncular but, now that they were in a sense colleagues, he was becoming less formal. He accepted the question without any trace of annoyance. "I played rugby for years without a scratch and then got bowled over and kicked in the face by a man I was trying to arrest for fraud. It happens that way, sometimes – it's the unexpected that catches one out. I've been offered corrective surgery but I keep it this way to remind my superiors of my devotion to duty. Also, I'm terrified of the surgeon's knife. Which reminds me. Knife. On the way out, I've put together a knife, fork, spoon, mug – the Teletubbies, is that all right? – and two plates. I couldn't spare a kettle but there's a small saucepan. I'll expect them back undamaged and preferably washed when you've managed to stock up."

"That's very kind and thoughtful of you." She sensed

that too much gratitude would have embarrassed him and sought for a change of subject. "I'm sure you're not really afraid of surgery," she said. "But don't have your nose put back the way it was. You look better the way you are."

He looked confused for a moment and she thought that she might have put her foot in it. Then he smiled again. "You think so?"

"I'm sure of it. But that's only a personal opinion and what do I know?"

"You've got to be a better judge than I am – I only see it front-on when I'm shaving and then not to notice. If I had been thinking of surgery, I'd certainly have cancelled it. And now, we must move."

He carried her heavy camera case, without apparent effort, out to his car. This was an inconspicuous mid-range saloon, not new and not old, not much of anything noticeable, an appropriate detective's car, she thought, but tidy and clean inside. The engine was brisk but quiet.

The scene of the fire was like a missing tooth in a beautiful face. The calm suburban street was broad and lined with expensive houses – appreciating investments as well as privileged homes – but it was now scarred by the soot-stained ruin, open to the sky. The gaudy fire appliances had gone, replaced by a smaller Fire Service van and another from the police plus several cars. The site was taped off and guarded against any risk of interference with the evidence.

Two fireman and a constable seemed eager to act as lady's maids as Jenny was fitted out with protective clothing from the vans. She needed to wear two extra pairs of socks before her small feet would fit the available boots. She joined a small group of similarly protected figures and was introduced to Station Officer Purbright from the Fire Service and a formidable lady, a Mrs Morrissey, from the Forensic Science Laboratory.

"I'm given to understand," Mrs Morrissey said, "that you were one of the first on the scene and that you took the photographs that appeared in today's press. Is that correct?" Jenny said that it was. "In your opinion, were the colours as reproduced in the *Tidings* a true representation?"

"I certainly didn't notice any discrepancy," Jenny said. "I can produce better prints when I get my negatives back."

"That could be useful. Now, let's have a general poke around."

Jenny set about taking shots of the whole scene, carefully noting down the content of each frame. She soon stopped noticing the reek of destruction. Most of the exterior walls were standing and had been pronounced stable, but the roof and the intermediate floors were down and the internal partitioning had burnt. Much of the structural timber and furniture had been consumed but the shell was cluttered with pieces of charcoal-coated timber, ash, piping and conduit. The water tank and a bath lay beside the remains of the central-heating boiler but only traces remained of other baths which had been of acrylic composition.

From time to time she was called on to pick her way through ashes and debris or to scramble over the heaped debris in order to photograph apparently meaningless details – the ends of wires or the pattern of cracks in a pane of glass. Mrs Morrissey and the Station Officer called for her services whenever they were collecting samples into glass bottles and nylon bags, but mostly she was left to her own devices.

The remains of the front door, after the attentions of the fireman, had almost burned away but the mortise lock was lying roughly where the doormat would have been, with the key beside it. She photographed them both.

They had worked for two hot, suffocating hours before she heard Mrs Morrissey's voice say, "As far as I'm concerned, your men can start to sift the ashes. Let's have a confab. You too, young woman – Miss Ambleside, is it?"

"Ambleton," Jenny said humbly.

"Same difference."

A group of men armed with trowels and sieves went to work at one end of the shell. Jenny joined the trio outside the ruin. There was a general removing of hard hats and opening of hot protective clothes.

"This one's going to go down as 'origin unknown'," Station Officer Purbright said. "In my opinion, that is. It's a puzzler. Miss Ambleton, confirm the evidence of your photographs and of my officers. What was the scene when you arrived?"

"The whole ground floor was alight," Jenny said, "and the upper floor was filled with smoke."

"Colour of smoke?" Mrs Morrissey snapped.

The question took Jenny by surprise. "I didn't notice anything out of the ordinary. My photographs show it as grey."

The group lost interest in Jenny.

"There are none of the usual suspicious signs," Mr

Purbright said. "No smell of petrol, for instance. And yet, many signs could have been lost in such total destruction. And such wholesale destruction is suspicious in itself. How did the whole ground floor become alight at the same time? No point of origin. Not even a radius of error. It's as if it all started simultaneously."

"That," boomed Mrs Morrissey, "is why I asked about the colours. There are many accelerants other than petrol and they do not all leave a smell behind for fire officers to notice. Reducing agents – oxidising agents, in fact. The halogen elements of fluorine and chlorine, for instance. Sodium or potassium nitrate. But all of those would produce brown fumes. Then there are sodium and potassium chlorate—"

"Now you're talking," said the Station Officer thoughtfully. "We had a case a couple of years ago. A young man who worked for a landscaping firm. He'd been spraying sodium chlorate solution as a weedkiller, on the site for a gravel car park. He must have sprayed some onto his clothes where it dried. He got on the bus to go home and lit a cigarette. He was badly burned and so was the man sitting next to him."

"Well," Mrs Morrissey said, "the bright yellow colour of the flames in the photographs suggests the presence of sodium. We'll have to wait and see what your men find and what chromatography and spectrometry can tell us. Of course, if sodium chlorate was used, most of the residue would be common salt, and I can't see any of us going into court and arguing that the presence of salt in an old dwelling has any significance. Superstitious people could have been throwing salt over their shoulders for years."

"Excuse me," Jenny said. The others fell silent and looked at her. "Perhaps I'm speaking out of turn," she said, "but you mentioned weedkiller."

"And the householder owns a garden centre," DS Welles said kindly. "We do know that. It doesn't make him guilty of anything."

"All right," said Jenny. She could feel herself flushing. She nearly decided to hold her tongue but she made one more effort. "So I'm an idiot. But there's something I'd like to show you all the same, because I think you've got a murder on your hands. Then if I'm talking nonsense I'll stop bugging you and stay quiet while the grown-ups are speaking."

There was a moment of perturbed silence. Mrs Morrissey seemed to swell. Jenny waited for something to burst and spill flesh all over the street. Then, quite mildly, the lady said, "What do you want to show us? We don't have to go back into that hell-hole, do we?"

"Only as far as the front door, when we're ready. I was trying to photograph any potentially significant details without disturbing anything. The front door lock is just lying there, chopped by the firemen and with most of the timber burnt away. The key was lying beside it. For the sake of a record photograph I thought that I might be forgiven if I put the key into the lock for a moment. But it just won't go."

Mr Purbright frowned. "You can't expect a lock to work when it's been heated up and squirted with foam," he said.

"You don't understand," Jenny said desperately. "It's not just that the key wouldn't turn. It wouldn't go into the lock at all. It's too big. So I had a look at the key which is still in the back door. It's a bigger lock and a smaller key."

"You're sure?" the DS asked quietly.

"Positive. Look for yourselves."

"We will, of course. Assuming that you're right, what do you read into it?"

Jenny was surprised to be asked a question which seemed to be more his concern than hers and wondered if it was some kind of trap. The DS recognised her hesitation. "You've had a few minutes to think about it," he said. "The concept is brand new to us. If it led you to conclude that we have a murder on our hands, you must have added some reasoning."

Jenny took a deep breath and soldiered on. "I think that somebody meant the fire to happen and didn't want Mrs Oliver, if that's who it is, to get out. The windows are fitted with security locks and I don't see any of the keys around. Double glazing's notoriously difficult to break. I think that somebody put the front-door key in the back-door lock and dropped the back-door key just inside the front door. Then he locked the front door with a spare key and went off. Like that, the scene would seem quite normal but if she made it downstairs she still couldn't get out. That's the only way that I can see it." She stopped and waited for the scorn and derision to burst over her.

But the others were nodding. "I noticed the lack of keys for the window latches," the Station Officer said. "It made me wonder. But householders often do remove them. There's little point having security locks if the first person to cut a hole in the glass can reach in and unlock the window."

The group moved to what remained of the front door. Station Officer Purbright squatted down with a cracking of joints. "No doubt about it," he said. "This key does not belong to this door."

"This is a viable theory and the first piece of constructive evidence we've come up with," Mrs Morrissey said. "It could link up all the anomalies. We'll have to see whether the searchers come up with anything that could have been part of a timing device – or a booby trap, of course. I'd better get back to the lab and check over these samples."

"Hold on a moment," DS Welles said. "Everything that's just been said presupposes that this is a one-off, as a method of murder or to conceal a crime, and not part of the previous series."

"It may have been intended to seem part of the series," Mrs Morrissey said. "Or it may have been part of the previous series and pretending not to be."

"Hold on a moment," said the DS unhappily. "Why would anybody do such a thing?"

"Somebody may have had this one in mind all along but set the earlier fires to distract from this one, if this fire should be recognised as arson. It's unlikely to fool you or me, but you can imagine what a defence lawyer could make of the existence of a prior arsonist. But those possibilities are for you to worry about, not for me, thank God! It's a pity that we don't have photographs of the rubbernecks at the previous fires. It's a rare arsonist who doesn't get a kick out of watching the results of his handiwork. And other fires, come to that. I refer, of course, to those arsonists who do it for fun, not the ones who have a more normal motive."

"But I have photographs," Jenny said. "At least, I don't know which fires you're treating as suspicious, but I photographed the watchers at Westerlink's and at the paint and varnish place and the paperworks. And here, of course. I think that Charlie, the night duty photographer at the *Tidings*, has been at one or two others."

"What a little treasure you're turning out to be," Mrs Morrissey said cheerfully. She was at least two inches shorter than Jenny but Jenny decided to let it go. The scientist turned to the DS. "If the same face keeps turning up, see if he fits the profile. You know what I mean – a loner, low intelligence, history of childhood antisocial behaviour, father absent and so on and so forth. If not, then my alternative theory may make a starting point. Somebody seems to want to talk to you. I'm off to look at my samples." With remarkable energy, considering her bulk, she trotted to a parked BMW and drove off, still in her protective overalls.

The man being held at bay by one of the guarding constables and trying to catch the eye of the DS was the bereaved Mr Oliver. Welles nodded to the constable, who let him through. Jenny noticed that his eyes were red-rimmed and he was badly shaved.

Mr Oliver wasted no time on greetings. "According to the paper, arson's suspected," he said. "Is that true?"

"It's a possibility," the DS admitted.

"Well, I want to know what you're doing about it."

Jenny offered her neighbour – and friend, she had decided – a burst of silent sympathy. Circumstances were manoeuvring him into a very difficult position. As a bereaved husband and dispossessed householder, Mr Oliver was presumably due all the consideration that the Force could offer; but Jenny's revelation and the subsequent discussion combined to suggest that he was also the most likely suspect. DS Welles, she guessed, was only with difficulty restraining himself from asking Mr Oliver what the hell he thought he would be doing about it.

Station Officer Purbright came to his aid. "The ashes are only now cool enough for a search to begin. The lady who just left is a forensic scientist and we'll have to wait for her report."

Mr Oliver made waving-away motions. He turned on DS Welles. "That's only half an answer. You're the detective, aren't you?" he said. "My wife died, my home's destroyed, I've lost the lot and now I hear that there may have been a criminal involvement. I want to know what *you*'re doing about it *now*."

Jenny saw the DS cast about for some sop that he could offer the man without at the same time accusing him. As clearly as though the thoughts had been written on a balloon above his head she saw him consider and discard most of what had been said that afternoon and settle instead on a comparative irrelevancy. "Among other actions, we shall be gathering up photographs taken at the scenes of several recent fires. An arsonist usually stays to watch it burn, so any face that turns up more than once is suspect, especially if it was seen here last night."

Mr Oliver glanced at Jenny without seeming to recognise her. "Is that so?" he said. "Well, I wish you joy of it."

"We'll keep you informed," the DS said. "Do we know where to find you?"

"My neighbour – *my former* neighbour – kindly put me up for the night. I'll be booking into a hotel today. I'll let you know which one." He turned and walked away.

DS Welles surreptitiously wiped his brow. "You've photographed the locked windows?"

"All of them," Jenny said.

"Great!" said the DS. "We'll have to see whether the searchers turn up any window keys and if so where. Next, you can take shots of me bagging those door locks and keys. And then," he told Jenny, "you and I had better go and make a report to the powers that be."

The *powers that were* consisted of a plain-clothes Detective Inspector Largs, a beefy bull of a man with a permanent sneer, whom DS Welles seemed to treat with cautious respect. Jenny and the DS were closely questioned, seated across from the DI at a table in a room in the Police HQ where half a dozen officers, some uniformed and some not, were busying themselves with telephones, papers and, in one instance, a computer.

In reporting, the Detective Sergeant confessed his own initial doubts and gave full credit to Jenny for her observation. It seemed to her that, as he spoke, he arranged the facts logically and laid them out as if for a museum exhibit with a precision that she could never have attempted. His methodical exposition convinced even Jenny, who had held doubts about her own reasoning, but DI Largs listened with an air of disbelief. His questions were snapped out as if to ward off any chance of sloppiness or evasion. He glowered, poked the carefully and separately bagged locks and keys with the end of a pencil and grunted.

Jenny was sure that she was about to be cast into outer darkness and that her friend and neighbour would blame her for his disgrace. It therefore came as a surprise when Mr Largs suddenly said, "You seem to be on to something. We'll see what the lab report and the photographs reveal. Meantime, we'll need open minds but the obvious suspect is this Mr Oliver. It's much too early to pull him in. Not going to skip the country, is he?"

"Very unlikely," the DS said. "He'd be abandoning some substantial business interests and he seems to have lost everything else. I don't think he'd fancy starting again from scratch in some foreign field. As far as he's concerned, we're only interested because we're wondering whether this is one of the series. That's why, when he asked what we were doing about it, I mentioned comparing the photographs of the rubbernecks at the various fires."

"Well done," the DI said grudgingly, surprising Jenny even more. Mr Largs had not struck her as the type of man who would be given to handing down accolades. "Tomorrow, we should have at least a preliminary report from the lab. I know Mrs Morrissey of old. Formidable old bat. She'll swear blind that the work's going to take a fortnight but if the case is worth it she'll work all night. And the photographs. Going to 'come out', are they?" he snapped at Jenny.

Jenny held her voice from going up into a squeak. "Of course," she said coldly. She wondered what mistakes she might have made. At least, she told herself, with a single lens reflex she could not have left the lens cap on without knowing it. And her freshly cut hair could not have blown in front of the lens.

"We may also have some gleanings from the fire site," the DS said.

"True. I'll go and brief the Super and we'll meet again tomorrow. Fix a time when that Fire Officer can come along." A smile appeared lopsidedly on his broad face. "And well done, young lady. That was good observation. We'll have to get you on the Force. Or marry you to one of our detectives." His twisted smile extended to embrace both sides of his face and he glanced from one to the other of them.

Jenny and the Detective Sergeant were very quiet on the way home. At last, he said, "If Mr Largs is determined to play Cupid and marry us off, you'd better call me Bob."

"Does he always get what he wants?" Jenny asked.

"Usually. I think you can count on having more work put your way. An intelligent and observant photographer can be an asset to any team and he knows it."

"Well, goody goody!" Jenny said without enthusiasm.

Bob Welles took his eyes off the road for a moment to glance at her. "Don't be put off more than a little by his manner," he said gently. "I've got to know him well, this last year or two, and I think that I owe him for my promotion. He's a tiger and if you do something stupid he can strip the hide off your back with his tongue; but most of that gruffness is designed to get the utmost out of his men and the rest is to cover up the fact that, underneath it all, he really cares. And he's a damn good copper with an almost unbroken series of successes behind him."

Jenny decided that if DI Largs had been good to Bob she would forgive him his grouches. His archness might prove a little more difficult.

Jenny ran her films to the photo laboratory and was promised her prints first thing in the morning. She caught the shops before they closed and made herself a late supper. Ashes and the smell of smoke clung to her. She had a leisurely bath and lay down on her bed in her old sleeping bag.

Exhaustion, following her truncated sleep of the previous night, carried her into oblivion undisturbed by dreams of faces at windows. She awoke, refreshed, as the traffic noises, muffled by the double glazing, built up outside. She was still sure that she smelled of smoke, so she bathed again and found another set of clean clothes from one of her cardboard cartons. She was scraping the bottom of the barrel where clothes were concerned. One more dirty day and she would be reduced to wearing her old gymslip, but at least she was decent in time to let in the carpet fitters. She had forgotten to order milk, so she had breakfast, of a sort, at the café beside the fire station before going to fetch her prints. A period of fine weather had broken and rain had set in. She crossed the streets under her small umbrella, dodging the spray from passing cars. In the jeep, she took a quick look at her prints. They were all bright and sharp. DI Largs would have no reason to vent his sarcasm on her.

Back at the flat, the carpet fitters were well ahead with the work. She told them to let themselves out and lock the door behind them.

The conference was called for mid-morning. She had

a little time in hand before Bob Welles was due to collect her. She sat out in the jeep with a copy of the *Tidings*. The supposed arsonist was still a major story. The correspondence columns held letters on the lines of What Are Our Police Doing About It? The question was answered in an editorial which announced that the police would be studying photographs taken at recent fire scenes. Arsonists, it was explained, invariably watched the outcome of their efforts and often other fires as well. The police would be looking for faces which featured more than once. Jenny wondered who had given the *Tidings* the story.

So, it seemed, did Detective Inspector Largs. This became clear as soon as they arrived for the conference. Gone was the benevolent ogre of the previous day. He had a copy of the *Tidings* before him and if it had not already been flat, the pounding that he was giving it would certainly have flattened it. The dozen or so officers in the cluttered room looked ready to dive under the tables.

Jenny denied emphatically that she had leaked the news, pointing out that, had she done so, she would have made sure that her name and her new profession were mentioned. This argument was accepted as convincing. Mr Largs' suspicions switched to the officers who had been in the room the previous evening, until Bob Welles mentioned that he had given the information to Mr Oliver, in the presence of Station Officer Purbright and possibly within earshot of a number of neighbours, any of whom might have told any number of others. Mr Purbright, refusing to be drawn, merely smiled and shook his head. The subject was allowed to lapse but clearly it would not be forgotten. Mr Largs made it more than clear that leaks from any unit under his leadership would not be tolerated.

It was reported that Mrs Morrissey had not yet found anything of significance. The searchers at the site, now being hampered by the rain which was turning the ash into porridge, had fared little better although it would not be known whether any significant finds had been made among the distorted or half-melted artefacts so far recovered until the search was completed and the discoveries could be studied in their overall context. The conference was therefore limited to bringing those present up to date with the probability of murder by arson. Jenny, made nervous by twenty or so faces, some solemn and some frankly lecherous, explained her discovery of the keys, which raised a murmur of interest.

Although the assumption was that a different arsonist was responsible, the same team, possibly augmented, would investigate. Superintendent Somebody-or-Other (Jenny failed to catch the name) would take personal charge, DI Largs said, if he ever brought himself to return from his conference in Paris.

At that point, when he was about to start allocating specific tasks to individuals, the Detective Inspector realised that an unauthorised civilian was among the officers present. He tried to dismiss Jenny to go and label her photographs in another room. Jenny raised the perfectly valid objection that she had photographed whatever she was told to photograph without, usually, having the least idea of its significance. "For instance," she said, "I photographed lots and lots of burnt wires.

How do I label those? Just 'Wires'? I'll need some help."

"I'll go with her," Bob Welles offered. (There were some nudges and winks.) "I can catch up later."

"Very well." Mr Largs nodded graciously. If there was a faint suggestion of Bless-you-my-children, Jenny managed to ignore it.

They adjourned into what she discovered was more usually an interview room and spread the photographs, in sequence, on the table. The DS produced labels and they began work. The significance of the wires, she discovered, was that the pointed ends and adhering insulation indicated heat arriving from outside, whereas a short circuit, one of the commonest causes of house fires, would have resulted in a beaded end to the wire and 'sleeving' of the insulation. They worked on. It was a long job, but between the DS's knowledge and Jenny's notes they usually managed to complete an acceptable text, inscribed onto a label in his meticulous script. They broke for a surprisingly good lunch in an institutional canteen. Jenny paid for her own and Bob told her to include it with her expenses.

They resumed work. In one or two instances they had to leave labels wholly or partially blank for Bob Welles to complete after conferring with Station Officer Purbright. It was late afternoon before he stretched and said, "That seems to be it. I'll run you home."

"You'll let me know if anything interesting happens?"

"If it seems right and proper."

They ducked through the rain to his car. Jenny checked to see that her big camera case was still in the back. Bob had been surprised when she insisted on bringing it along.

"If I don't," she said, "Martians will land somewhere along our route. This is my livelihood."

Bob chuckled. She seemed to make him laugh a lot, which she supposed was better than no reaction at all. There were, disappointingly, no excitements in their journey. "No Martians," the DS said as he pulled up. "I'll bring your case in."

Jenny went ahead under her umbrella.

She unlocked the door to her flat. The carpet fitters had gone. The sitting room looked much better, with her few pieces of furniture set out on wall-to-wall carpet instead of bare boards. But the carpet looked different, paler than she had expected and almost dusty. If the carpet had gathered so much dust in some warehouse, surely the fitters would have vacuumed it up?

She stepped forward. Near the door, a 50p coin on the floor caught her eye. Was this the carpet fitters' idea of a 'lucky penny'? She bent over the coin. As she did so, her umbrella fell open.

There was a crack like a pistol shot and a *Whoomph!* Heat licked around her and the room was full of heat and fumes. Stunned and bemused, she staggered back into the doorway.

Strong arms gripped her around the waist and swung her aside.

Six

In times of crisis, the mind has more important tasks than remembering. Jenny realised later that her recollections of the day from that point onward were patchy.

Bob said, "Burnt?" and she said, "Yes." She was dragged by one arm, almost thrown into a blue and white bathroom and told, "Whatever smarts, cold water on it." She had enough control of herself to run cold water into the bath. The smarting, barely noticed at first, was becoming pain but it seemed to be confined to her brow, ankles and left hand and wrist. She knelt in the bath and put her face down.

Bob must have been on the phone. She could hear his voice, rapid, firm and controlled. "All three," he said. And then, "No, cancel the Fire Service, they're here already. Ambulance first, then police." He gave the address.

Jenny thought of taking off her wristwatch but her wrist was too tender to touch. It was only a fake, a cheap copy of a Cartier watch. She had bought it in the Caribbean, in the company of the French officer. He had never replied to her one letter. She let it drown.

After that came a blank. Then Bob seemed to have

helped her out of the bath just as the ambulance arrived. She had a lucid moment while practicalities came rushing at her. "Look after my cameras," she said. "Please."

"Don't worry about it."

"The fire . . ."

"It's out already."

"Would you tell my insurance company?"

"Who are they?"

"Norfolk General."

She was whisked out to the ambulance. The hall seemed to be full of firefighters and equipment. The smell of burning was everywhere but the men seemed to be moving around unhurriedly so she accepted that the emergency was over. Except for herself, she realised suddenly. She was the emergency now.

Bob stayed behind. Part of her resented his desertion of her but the other part knew that he was right.

Another blank and, seconds later it seemed, she was wrapped in a blanket and waiting in a cubicle in Accident and Emergency and her burns hurt like hell. A nurse came and undressed her tenderly and put her into a hospital gown. Her clothes had been burnt in patches and then soaked. None of her outer garments would be wearable again but on her behalf the nurse managed to rescue the contents of her anorak pockets – the two pairs of socks, a few coins, a handkerchief and three partly melted, unexposed films.

A doctor arrived, a jolly, bustling young man with red hair and a snub nose. "Well, now. What happened to you?"

Explaining would be too much bother. "Don't know."

He examined her. "Whatever it was, it could have been

serious. You've got off comparatively lightly. Only the extremities seem to have caught it."

"My clothes were damp and I had a wet umbrella in front of me."

"That would explain it. Keep the umbrella and have it framed, it must be your lucky talisman. We'll have to keep you in for a day or two."

"Can't I just phone for clean, dry clothes and go and suffer at home?" she asked, wondering as she spoke where home was now.

The doctor shook his curly red head. "We'll have to keep you under observation, for shock or infection. Burns get infected very easily."

She had never cared very much about her appearance but suddenly it became important to know. "Will I be much marked?"

He looked at her again through a man's eyes. Then he was once again the doctor. "I doubt it," he said. "You've lost some hair but most of it should grow back. If you wear it in a fringe, nobody'll ever know that there's about a square centimetre missing. The scarring should heal naturally."

She was satisfied. She had always had a fringe but she seemed to have mislaid it for the moment.

Somebody must have fed her a painkiller because she slept, woke to have her dressings changed and slept again. The next time she awoke, in a single-bed room, her parents were waiting patiently. Her mother, usually quite as imposing as Mrs Morrissey, was tearful. Her father, who was mentally strong despite a fragile appearance, was in an I-told-you-so mood. Somebody had already given them some details but they were bursting with questions. She pretended to fall asleep again, just to be rid of them.

Her burns woke her periodically during the night but she was awake and alert before the night staff began their preparations for a handover. She was washed very gently and her dressings were changed again. She did justice to a better breakfast than she could have managed at home. The word had gone round that she had lost everything in the fire (an exaggeration, but not much more than the truth), so by diverse means a hairbrush and other toiletries had been found for her. Somebody had even found a container for the contact lenses which had survived the fire undamaged in her eyes. Flexing her wrist still set her skin on fire but with the help of a friendly nurse she managed to make herself presentable.

For this she was grateful because, some time later, Bob Welles, capitalising on his status as a police officer, arrived and settled himself in the only visitor's chair. To her surprise and pleasure, he brought her flowers and even persuaded a nurse to find a vase. He was looking much neater than usual, in well-pressed flannels and a sports jacket with a white shirt open at the neck. She decided that as soon as she was out of hospital she would buy him a scarf, a cravat, an ascot, whatever they called it, as a substitute for the tie which he evidently disliked. He had her sympathy. A tie had figured largely in her school uniform and she had disliked the constriction intensely.

"Which do you want first?" he asked. "The good news or the better news?"

She peered at him. "Are you just trying the cheer me up? Or isn't there any bad news?"

"If there is, I'm not the bearer of it. For a start, I've had a word with the doctor who admitted you. He says that you'll be out in a few days and your beauty won't be spoiled."

Jenny was startled that anybody should use the word in connection with herself. "That old thing?" she said carefully. She would have liked him to expand on the subject but found herself unable to ask.

"Don't knock it. You may be glad of it some day. And your hair should grow back, give or take a very little. Why do you wear it so short?"

"I know it doesn't suit me short, but long hair blows in front of the camera."

"You should wear it in a ponytail. Then you'd have it for when you want it. Why," he asked suddenly, "are you looking at me in that suggestive manner? I'd help you anyway without the lewd expression."

She fought back a temptation to giggle. "I can't put my contact lenses in and out one-handed and I can't see you properly without half-closing my eyes. Would you ask my mother to bring my old spectacles in, please?" She quoted the phone number. "I apologise if I'm using you as an errand-boy."

"It's no trouble. Use me all you want. Next, your flat isn't as badly damaged as it might have been. One of the fire officers was looking across the street and saw the flare-up as it happened, so they were on the scene before it took hold. Also, your carpet had been flameproofed, unlike the one at Mr Oliver's house, and plasterboard behaves very well in a fire."

"So does a wet umbrella," Jenny said. "Mine fell open as I bent down."

"And your clothes were damp. You've been very lucky."

"You didn't get any burns, did you?" she asked.

"Nothing. You're going to stay on?"

The question took her by surprise. "At the flat? Yes, of course I'm going to stay."

"That's good," he said without inflection. "I thought that the fire might have given you a horror of the place and that you were going to run back to mother."

"Believe me, mothers like mine are not for running back to."

He raised an eyebrow but made no other comment. "Your carpets are spoiled and you'll need new decoration and furniture and some woodwork replaced. I've notified your insurers and they'll send you a claim form through me. You're covered for arson and malicious damage?"

Jenny thought back two whole days. It seemed more like a year. "Yes," she said at last. "Definitely. My mind was already on arson when I fixed up the policy, so I checked."

"Good. I'll bring you up a colour chart. If you choose colours, I'll have the work put in hand. Do you want the same carpet again?"

Things were moving too fast. "I don't know," she said unhappily. "I chose the first one to go with the colours that were already on the walls. If I'm starting again from scratch . . .'

"I'll get a swatch for you to choose from."

Jenny was not used to so much consideration and she found that it troubled her. "Don't think I'm not grateful," she said awkwardly, "but before I let you go to so much trouble, please tell me why you're being so helpful."

He met her eyes. His manner had been light and teasing as though he was trying to steer her mood back towards its usual levity, but now he looked serious. "You're a neighbour. I like you. You need help. And if those aren't enough reasons, I feel responsible," he said slowly.

"That's rubbish! How could you be responsible?"

"I gave you the job, I took you out to Mr Oliver's house and I announced to the world that we were going to study the photographs of the spectators at the fires. Everybody must have seen your name under those photographs that were published, so it wouldn't take a genius to work out who held most of the negatives. The secretary at the *Tidings* remembers an unidentified caller asking for your address, about midday yesterday. They gave the caller your new address. They probably thought that they were doing you a favour and sending you a client. I think this fire may have been set in the hope of eradicating the negatives."

"Then it wasn't very successful," Jenny said. "If the caller had enquired more closely he – it was a he?"

"The secretary couldn't remember."

"The caller would have found that I was only just moving in. And even if I'd finished moving, he wouldn't have got the negatives. One of the attractions of the flat, for me, was that the brick shed at the back goes with it and I'm going to make it into a store for my negatives. I have a cabinet coming but it isn't here yet so most of my negatives are at home, those that aren't with my agent or with *Tidings*. Dan Mandible – my agent – warned me never to let my negatives out of my hands and I seem to have been scattering them all over the city."

Even without her contact lenses, his delighted smile made her feel warm. "Then I can collect them?" he asked.

"I don't know that you can. I . . . I take it that my computer was destroyed?"

"Yes, I'm afraid so."

She pulled a face. "Norfolk General are going to love me. I'd only had it a week. And I hadn't even used my darkroom equipment. I'll have a hell of a job finding the right negatives without the computer. I doubt if a stranger could do it at all. Unless . . ."

"Unless?"

"My mother was helping me with the indexing. She's better at computers than I am. She uses one regularly as secretary of the local antiquarian society. She may have kept a disk or a printout. I'll ask her. But, either way, I think you'll have to wait until I'm up and about again. How urgent is it?"

He raised his hands in a gesture of uncertainty. "We can't tell. Not very, if the threat has frightened him off for the moment. The case – or perhaps two cases – is or are a muddle. Mrs Morrissey hasn't finished work yet but already she's prepared to swear that your flat and Mr Oliver's house were both fired using sodium chlorate as the reducing agent, probably with sugar added where particular intensity was wanted. Sugar plus chlorate equals one of the primitive explosives used by terrorists. That's the kind of chemical equation they teach us in the police these days. That seems to link the two fires closely together. On the other hand, as I said once before, the previous fires were clumsy, petrol-and-a-match jobs, or just a match in the case of the cardboard boxes. Quite different. Unless one of Mrs Morrissey's far-fetched theories is correct, that seems to give us two separate series of arson attacks.

"Malicious fires are started for a number of reasons. We can discount an employee with a grievance. We can forget about jealousy and terrorism, and probably insurance fraud. The earlier fires have the hallmark of the weak-minded person who gets a kick, probably a sexual kick, out of watching the results. Those are the fires which the culprit is most likely to stick around and watch. The Oliver fire is quite different. It was more sophisticated. And there was a fatality. It was a one-off and the obvious suspect has an alibi – which may prove to be worthless. We've found no evidence of a timer or a booby trap at either place yet, but there was certainly nobody hanging around your flat with a match. Yet an announcement which, logically, should have the starter of the first series of fires shaking in his shoes provokes an apparent response from the person who arranged the Oliver fire."

"So Mrs Morrissey could be right after all." An uncomfortable question had been nagging at Jenny. "Was I meant to die in the fire?" she asked

His eyes weighed her up. "Would the thought worry you?"

"It's a difficult idea to get hold of, that somebody may have tried to incinerate me. But no, don't think so. Not worried in the sense of afraid. Not if you tell me that I'm in no danger now."

"Then I'll put it this way. I think that, at the least, your death would have been considered a bonus. After all, if he searched the flat and couldn't find your negatives among all those boxes and boxes of treasures, he could have torched the place while he was there. Or there are any number of timer devices possible. A gelatine capsule filled with nitric acid, for one. When the acid has eaten through the gelatine and reaches the chlorate, up she goes. Yet he must have gone to the trouble of rigging a booby trap for the whole caboodle to go *whoosh!* just as you walked in."

"Baited with a fifty-pee coin," Jenny said. "I'm insulted. He could at least have made it a pound."

Bob Welles gave a shout of laughter that brought a nurse to look in and frown warningly at him. "I'm glad you're taking it so well," he said, still grinning. "Just how the booby trap worked we have yet to puzzle out. But, to answer your other point, you're in no immediate danger. There was a WPC outside your door all night. We can't keep that degree of protection up for much longer, but we shouldn't have to. The best defence will be to let it be known that we already have all the photographs we need—"

Before he could finish, he was interrupted by preparations for the doctor's rounds and it was made clear that he was no longer exempt from the restrictions on visiting hours. "I'll go and get something to eat," he said. "There's a café in the basement and I don't know when I'll have time again. I'll be back."

Jenny was tidied. The doctor arrived with a retinue of students, nurses and everybody, probably including, Jenny thought, the window cleaner. Her burns were dressed again. They hurt a little less each time. She

107

must have figured late on the doctor's rounds because her lunch followed almost on his heels.

True to his word, Bob Welles returned, but by then the afternoon visiting hours had arrived and with it Mr and Mrs Ambleton. They were burdened with much fruit and fruit juice, Jenny's old spectacles (found at the back of a drawer after a protracted hunt) and a great cloud of anxious curiosity. The *Tidings* that morning had reported the fire and, evidently quoting from a police press release, announced that the police were treating the fire as suspicious. It was left to the reader to infer any connection with the previous fires. Jenny, uncertain how to proceed, was parrying their questions as well as she could when Bob came back. Their curiosity, and that of Mrs Ambleton in particular, was immediately transferred. Bearing in mind her promise, Jenny introduced him as "Bob Welles, my neighbour across the hall".

"You phoned me about Jenny's glasses," Mrs Ambleton said triumphantly. "I'd recognise that voice anywhere."

Apparently, the acquisition by their untidy tomboy daughter of a personable and grown-up boyfriend was of far greater interest than the incineration of her flat. Bob made himself agreeable to them, chatted patiently about several of Mrs Ambleton's hobby horses and, when visiting hours were over, escorted them down to their car, making only the most formal of farewells. Jenny was left to take what comfort she could from the fact that, as he left the room, he turned and winked at her.

* * *

It was the evening of the following day before Bob

Welles returned. Jenny spent much of the time looking
out of the window and trying to forget her discomfort.
The rain still fell, sometimes in sheets and sometimes
only in a drizzle. Usually she would have been depressed
by the view of a tightly regimented piece of garden being
beaten down and muddied by the downpour; but at least
she was spared the frustration of missing any fine weather
during her incarceration and she was comforted by the
fact that, but for the rain which had wet her jeans and
necessitated the use of her umbrella, her burns would
have been far worse. Rain, for the moment, was good
and the sun, representing fire, was bad.

Jenny was sitting up. She had borrowed a little
make-up from a friendly nurse who had resorted to
her room for a secret smoke at the temporarily open
window. The swathing of bandages around her head had
been replaced by a single band, resembling the sweatband
worn by tennis players, which almost hid her hair loss.
Contact lenses were still too troublesome to put in and
out, and even more so while she was liable to fall asleep
at any moment of the day and waken with her lenses dried
out and feeling like sandpaper. Glasses, Jenny thought,
gave her an approachable, girl-next-door look and also
lent her a possibly deceptive air of intelligence. Bob
was looking damp, tired and dispirited but he seemed
to brighten at the sight of her. He shed his hat, raincoat
and a heavy briefcase and took the visitor's chair. He
had brought flowers again.

She wanted to make him smile. "Do you want the
good news or the better news?" she asked.

He obliged her by smiling. "Either."

"The good news is that my mother does have a floppy

disk of my index and she brought it in this afternoon. It's on the locker. Do you have access to a computer or shall I get her to print it out for me?"

He picked up the small package and slipped it into his pocket. "I'll get it printed. What's the even better news?"

"The even better news is that they think I'll get out tomorrow. What's the matter?" she added. "Don't you want me to get better?" He had pursed his lips at her second announcement.

"I'm delighted that you're on the mend," he said. "I couldn't be more pleased. It's just . . . We think that you're safe in here. We don't know whether you'll be in any danger outside, but you'll be much more difficult to guard."

Jenny gave an ostentatious sigh. "One of my teachers told me that one should never, ever begin a sentence with the words, *But you said.*"

"Then I'll save you the need. But I said that one good thing was that any danger should be past as soon as it was generally known that we have our hands on all the crowd photographs that we need. And we can count on the *Tidings* to spread that news for us. I've never seen you with spectacles before," he added.

"I don't often wear them now. I prefer my contact lenses – spectacles get in the way when you're using a camera – but contacts are a damn nuisance in here. I've given up for the moment. You think I might be in danger because whoever-it-was laid a booby trap instead of using a timer?"

"We aren't even sure of that," he told her. "The searches at both houses have turned up almost nothing."

110

"Except that fifty-pee coin."

"Ah! Now, at that point we've had a stroke of luck. Confidential?"

"I'm treating everything I get from you as confidential. If I want to talk, I'll ask you first."

"I can't ask for more. I don't know what this means, if anything, but you can hold your head up again. He did value you at a pound. There were two fifty-pee coins, and two similar coins were found among the debris in the vicinity of the hall at the Oliver house. We think that they may have been on top of each other and that the upper one was flipped into the air. I found one inside your umbrella. It may lead to the answer or it may be the outcome of a mad coincidence. But Mrs Morrissey found traces of what she thinks, only thinks, may have been a percussive mixture – styphnate, I think she said – commonly used in cartridge primers." He paused dramatically.

"Go on," Jenny said. "Don't tease me."

"And caps for toy pistols! A sprinkling of caps between two coins, struck a sharp blow, could certainly set off sodium chlorate, especially with a little sugar added to the chlorate."

"That would explain the loud crack that I heard just before everything went hot."

"Which is all very well," Bob said, with a return of his gloom. "But a sharp blow would be needed to set it off. And unless you tell me that you jumped up and down on the coins, we haven't the faintest idea how it was done. We'd be laughed out of court if we tried for a conviction on what we've got just now. If we could find so much as the spring out of a mousetrap . . ."

It occurred to Jenny that her glasses might lend her more than a superficial look of intelligence. She was inspired. "There is one thing," she said.

"Yes?"

"You'd better ask Mrs Morrissey about this. But have you heard of ammonium iodide?"

His eyebrows went up. "No. I never was much for chemistry."

"It was one of my best subjects. But no way was this in the curriculum. I'd forgotten all about it, but I haven't always been the good little girl you see before you."

"I never supposed that you had. Far better to get rid of your devilment in childhood. Should I warn you that anything you say will be taken down and may be used in evidence?"

"We'll take it as read. Mrs Morrissey's word would carry more authority than mine. Dominic – my brother – and I used to make ammonium iodide for fun. You only need iodine crystals and concentrated ammonia solution. Mix them together, pour off the liquid and keep the precipitate. As long as it's wet, it's perfectly stable; but as soon as it dries it goes off bang at the slightest touch. Dominic let some dry on a glass slide once and he tried to lower a drop of water onto it. It went off and broke the slide, but he was all right. We used to put a little down on the floor at school if we wanted to disrupt the lessons. It created havoc and a lot of brown smoke but they never caught on."

With an effort, Bob contained his amusement. "I'm glad that I wasn't at your sort of school. Go on. Tell me what you're thinking."

"You'd better try this out for yourself or get Mrs

Morrissey to do it. This is what I think he may have done. He sprinkled his sodium chlorate around, with sugar where he wanted extra heat. He put down one fifty-pee coin, sprinkled a few caps on it, added the other coin and put a dollop of wet ammonium iodide on top. To be sure that it went off as soon as I walked in and before I had time to notice anything wrong, he could have led a piece of cotton from something fixed and across the ammonium iodide. That would be quite enough. Once it was dry, anyone stepping on or touching the cotton would set it off."

Bob sat, deep in thought, silent except for a drumming of two fingers on the bedside cabinet. "In the case of Mrs Oliver," he said, "the ground floor was on fire but she was still upstairs. We think that she was meant to be killed by smoke inhalation. According to her husband, she had a migraine and went to lie down. The prescription furnished by her doctor would have helped her to sleep for several hours."

Jenny's mind was suddenly racing. She hated what she was thinking but she was unable to stop. "If she was meant to die in her sleep, somebody could have dropped a match or used a timer of some sort. A booby trap of the kind I've been describing would mean that somebody wanted her to wake up and be burnt when she started moving around, not be burnt in her sleep. But that's horrible!"

"Sometimes people are horrible," Bob said gently.

"I suppose so. A thread could have run all the way from her bedroom and down the stairs, and you still wouldn't have found any traces of it after the fire, would you?"

"No," he said thoughtfully. "I don't suppose we would. I'll pass on the suggestion. It sounds quite unpleasantly feasible." He cogitated for a few seconds while Jenny maintained a respectful silence. When he spoke again, it was on a complete change of subject. "I got an electrician in to check your wiring. The plastic sockets require renewal. Otherwise it's all right."

"Shouldn't you have waited for the Norfolk General?"

"The wiring had to be checked, whatever your insurers say." He opened his briefcase. "I have some carpet samples and a colour chart. If you'll make up your mind what you want, I'll get estimates for your insurance company."

"You're very good to me," Jenny said in a small voice.

"Fair's fair. You're doing my job for me," he said gruffly.

"What nonsense! I just happened to know about ammonium iodide."

The Detective Sergeant made no answer. They settled down to a discussion of colour schemes.

* * *

The next day, Jenny was subjected to a series of hammer blows. The first was delivered by the doctor on his rounds. He tutted over her wrist. "This still isn't healing as I'd hoped," he said. "We'll have to go for a skin graft. It's only a small area but it will need a larger graft. I'll get Mr Morton to do it. He has a gap in his list tomorrow afternoon."

114

"Is he good?" Jenny asked suspiciously. She knew that there was usually a lengthy waiting list. Any surgeon who could take a non-urgent patient at a day's notice was suspect.

The doctor stiffened. In his view, it was not for a mere patient to ask that sort of question. "The best," he said.

"Then how does he come to have a gap in his list?"

The doctor hesitated. He avoided her eye. "Somebody cancelled," he said.

"You mean, they died?"

"I couldn't tell you."

Jenny was left more than normally depressed. In addition to her own impending operation and the delay to her escape from this boring confinement, she was on the burns ward and presumably Mr Morton was a specialist in burn surgery. From her own recent experience, she could imagine no more terrible ending than to die a lingering death from burns. Better by far to be put to sleep. The family dog, an Old English sheepdog full of years and losing its faculties, had been given a merciful release the previous year and at the time she had wondered why that privilege was reserved for animals and forbidden for their owners. She tried hard not to think about it but the very effort of heading her mind away from the subject kept bringing it back. She picked at her lunch, although this was to be her last food until the following evening.

The next blow fell shortly before the official hour for afternoon visiting. A small man in a dark suit came bustling in. He was very thin, with a pointed nose tinged with pink, and his eyes, Jenny noticed, were a very pale blue.

He handed her an envelope. "Norfolk General Insurance Company," he said briskly in a voice as sharp as his nose. "The letter explains. Sign here, please."

The paper on which Jenny was invited to sign her name was a receipt referring unspecifically to 'documents', followed by a tangle of legal and insurance jargon. "I don't understand," she said. "Is this my claim form?"

"The letter explains it all," he repeated. "Just sign."

"I only have one unbandaged hand," Jenny said. "Open the envelope for me, please."

"Quite unnecessary, I assure—"

A nurse, the one who used her room for a surreptitious smoke and with whom Jenny had chatted about life and love, was passing the doorway. Jenny called to her and the nurse used her scissors to open the envelope. Jenny's eye was first caught by a cheque. It seemed to be made out for a sum which she remembered as having been the amount of the premium on her domestic insurance. "You have a card?" she asked the man.

He looked uncomfortable. "Not on me."

Jenny skimmed through the letter.

Dear Miss Ambleton

With reference to the above policy, we understand that a fire occurred on the evening of the 8th instant, occasioning considerable damage to your flat and to the contents.

We were given to understand by the Press that this fire was considered by the Police to be of a

116

suspicious origin and this has been confirmed by a source within the Fire Service.

It is further noted that your policy had been in force for only two days before the fire referred to and it is reported that before finalising the policy you enquired specifically as to whether arson was included in the fire cover.

In the circumstances, this Company has no option but to consider any claim invalid and to cancel your insurance. Your premium is returned herewith.

Yours sincerely
J.Asquith
Branch Manager

Jenny began to boil. Using one hand and her teeth, she tore up the cheque and threw it at the man. "I'm not accepting my premium back," she said.

He nodded unemotionally. "That's up to you. I'll take back the receipt," he said flatly.

He made a move as if to snatch it. Jenny pushed it down among the bedclothes. "I'm keeping it," she said. "I want to know what I was asked to sign." The nurse had lingered out of curiosity. "You're a witness to what I've said," Jenny told her.

The nurse nodded. "I shan't forget."

"Nor shall I," the man said ominously. "You're being very foolish. You would be wise to forget the whole matter and write it off to experience." They heard his footsteps slap angrily as they faded along the corridor.

"I think you're meant to shake in your shoes," said the nurse. "But of course you're not in your shoes."

"If I'm shaking, it's with fury," Jenny said.

Minutes later, official visiting hours began. More footsteps moved in the corridor and there were voices, respectfully hushed.

Dan Mandible looked cautiously round the doorpost and then came in. "This is the right room, then," he said. Jenny noticed that he had brought none of the conventional gifts to the patient and that he looked unusually grim. He made only the most perfunctory enquiries after her recovery. He stood at the foot of her bed, erect and uneasy. "That photograph of the couple on board the ship," he said.

"The Olivers?"

"Unfortunately not. Listen, Jenny. I sold that photograph to the *Tidings* and several other papers as being a recent photograph of the couple. I sold it in good faith and on your say-so. Now Mr Oliver's lawyers have been insisting that he went on the cruise on his own and that the woman was no more than a casual acquaintance who he was surprised to meet on board. Being alone, they say, he was happy to squire her about by day, but that's as far as it went. They insist that he's been exposed to scandal, ridicule and police investigation by the publication of the photograph and that his businesses have lost money because of it. He wants a printed retraction and compensation or he'll sue for libel. The papers are printing a retraction and an apology and they seem inclined to pay some compensation and write the matter off. They will almost certainly look to us for recourse." He paused. "Do you have professional indemnity insurance?"

"No."

"No more do I. I never thought to need it in a retirement activity."

Jenny skin was prickling. Her mouth dried and she found that she was short of breath. She was sure that she could hear her own heartbeat. "He can't get away with that," she said at last. "Can he? He introduced her to me as his wife."

"You can prove that?"

"I don't know." She fought down her panic and tried to think calmly. "There weren't any witnesses to that particular conversation. Would it help if I produced more photographs of them together on the ship?"

"I doubt it. They could, as he maintains, quite innocently have gone around together by day and danced together in the evenings. He could say that his wife knew all about it. She isn't around to say anything different. If you could find other passengers who'd been told that she was his wife, that would be more to the point."

The scale of the task was more than Jenny could contemplate. "The passenger list?" she suggested.

"If it shows a Mr and Mrs David Oliver, that might do it. You have a copy?"

"I had a copy. I don't remember whether it's in one of the boxes I left at home, in which case it still exists, or one of the ones taken to the flat, in which case it doesn't. I'll ask my mother to hunt for it. Failing which, the cruise line might be able to furnish a copy."

Dan nodded without looking any happier. "It's worth a try, I suppose. But if they went aboard separately we're up the gum tree, and never mind what they got up to during the hours of darkness. In the meantime, I don't think any of the papers will touch your stuff with a barge pole. Outsiders letting them in for a libel action is one thing they never forgive."

It seemed that there was a thin time ahead. Which brought her mind back to her insurance claim. "How much do I have coming for those photographs?" she asked.

"About enough to pay for your carpets, if they cough up. They may hold onto it to set against the libel compensation."

Jenny scowled through her spectacles. "Have I got this right? You're talking about compensation which they decide to cough up at my expense and against my will? Can they get away with that?"

"If you're big enough and can afford top lawyers," Dan said gloomily, "you can get away with almost anything."

"That doesn't seem very fair."

"It isn't fair. But newspapers and insurance companies have the money and the lawyers to go to court. It's their decision whether they fight us or Mr Oliver and we may be the softer target. Whoever told you that life's fair was lying in his teeth."

"But suppose Mr Oliver turns out to be guilty of killing his wife?"

At last, Dan showed signs of brightening. "That could be quite a different ball game," he said. His mind went straight to the seller's market, not to litigation. "They'd be bidding against each other for your photographs."

That seemed to be carrying optimism too far. "It wouldn't exactly be a *cause célèbre*," Jenny protested.

"Have you been living in a darkroom all your life?"

Dan asked. "Haven't you noticed the basic rule of media exposure, that a story is only news if they have pictures of it? The better the pictures, the bigger the news."

Dan Mandible had hardly made his despondent way out before Bob Welles arrived with a small pot plant and the printout of Jenny's index of negatives, a document already eleven pages long. Jenny might be feeling like something that the cat had rejected but it would have been unfair to take it out on him. She forced a welcoming smile and told him that the plant would look splendid in her sitting room if she ever had a sitting room again. They settled down and she explained her system of indexing, ringing the numbers of negatives that might hold what he wanted.

"The sooner we get this over," Bob said, "the sooner I'll be able to feel happier about your safety. When are you getting out?" Sartorially he had progressed as far as a thin polo-neck, she noticed, and was beginning to look quite presentable.

"Not today after all," said Jenny. "They want to do a graft on my wrist." She managed to keep self-pity out of her voice. A small percentage of patients, she had been told, fail to come round from the anaesthetic. Just at the moment, she thought that she might enjoy being one of them.

Bob assumed a carefully sympathetic expression. "I'm sorry for your sake and I hope you'll soon recover, but just for the moment I'm glad that you'll be safe in here. Would you give me a note to your parents, authorising them to hand over your negatives to me?"

"If you'll hold the paper for me. But it isn't just my parents. The *Tidings* must still have some of my negatives. You'd better approach them through my agent. And the last crowd shots were in the same batch as my shots of the Oliver house."

"And where are those?"

"I left the whole packet in your incident room. Your Mr Largs took charge of them. They won't have made their way into my index yet, but there were enlargements. So you'll easily find what you want." Jenny moved uneasily. Her burns were nagging at her. "One of the first things my agent said to me was that I should never part with a negative and now I seem to be scattering them all over the place. I want everything back and in the same order." Her words reminded her of something. "I'm sorry about your plates and things," she added.

"I got them back, sooty but perfectly washable." He looked at her hard. "You don't seem to be your usual chirpy self."

Rather than break down, Jenny made an effort to pass off the moment. "No point burdening you with my problems. A trouble shared is a trouble doubled."

"That's more like your old self, but you're talking rubbish. Whatever it is, I can probably help."

Her parents would have sounded censorious or suspicious but Bob's tone was wholly kind and concerned. Jenny blinked back tears. She found herself pouring out the story of her woes.

Bob was inclined to dismiss the possibility of a libel action. "He'd never let it go that far. This is just a delaying tactic, to keep the media from harping on the scandal."

"He doesn't have to go to court," Jenny said miserably.

"My agent says that the papers are deciding to settle with him and then turn on us."

Bob's mind was on a different track. "We'd better keep an eye on the gentleman," he said. "He may be planning to skip after all. Don't worry too much. If and when we get to the stage of a prosecution, the photographs they won't print now will become valuable commodities."

"But I don't have any money *now*," Jenny pointed out. "I have about enough coming in – if it comes at all – to pay for the first lot of carpets, the ones that burned. If the insurance won't cough up, I've lost everything." Her voice broke.

"Give me that letter," Bob said grimly. "*And* the receipt. You've still got your flat and, whatever happens, it has to be repaired and redecorated. I'll set things in motion."

The flat might have to be sold, Jenny realised. The thought was followed by another. "My car!" she said. "It's still standing outside at the front, probably on bricks instead of wheels by now and covered with parking tickets."

"It'll be waiting when you want it," Bob said. "I moved it to the police garage."

This indication of thoughtfulness was almost the last straw. "Oh, Bob! I don't want you to get into trouble. Should you be spending so much time on my affairs?"

"The last instruction I had from Mr Largs was to look after you. I told you once before that under that abrasive exterior there was a gentle soul in hiding."

For some reason, the news that the large and galvanic Detective Inspector was concerned for her removed Jenny's last vestige of self-control. She felt the tears come.

Any other male of her acquaintance would have found some excuse to go for a walk, but Bob was made of sterner stuff. "Here, here," he said. He offered her a large, clean handkerchief although there were tissues at hand. "Nothing's ever that bad. Would a hug help?"

He may have thought that Jenny nodded, because he moved to sit beside her on the bed and she found herself wrapped in a respectful but comforting embrace. And thus they were discovered when Mr and Mrs Ambleton walked in, ten minutes later.

Only pride kept Jenny from hiding under the bedclothes from the roguish glances, but Bob was quite unabashed. He chatted pleasantly for a minute, only slightly modifying his clasp on her while Jenny broke the news of her impending operation and delayed release from hospital. She made no mention of any financial worries. The Ambletons, it transpired, already knew of Bob's position in the police. When he got up, Bob swept Mrs Ambleton away with him in order to claim Jenny's negatives, leaving Mr Ambleton to amuse Jenny alone.

"Very well thought of, your new boyfriend," he said.

"He is not my boyfriend," Jenny said slowly and distinctly. "He just happens to live across the hall from me. Because of that, he engaged me to take some photographs for the police. And that's probably why my flat was torched. I'll be just as happy to have my negatives taken away, before you suffer the same."

Mr Ambleton seemed not to have heard a word. "I spoke to a friend of mine, a superintendent," he said.

"Youngest detective sergeant on the force, your Bob, and already singled out for inspector."

"Well, bully for him!" Jenny said. Nobody seemed to want to discuss her operation.

Seven

The surgeon was a dour Scot whose face would have fragmented if he had ever smiled. He addressed Jenny as if she were an unruly class of students. In contrast, the anaesthetist was a jolly, younger man. He patiently explained every step of the planned procedures and was busy telling Jenny a mildly rude joke about two nurses and a chiropractor when she went under, missing the punchline.

She came to, back in her bed. Her heavily bandaged wrist hurt much more than before despite a heavy dose of painkillers and she had a new soreness on the inner side of her thigh at the donor site where the skin for the graft had been removed. She rather resented the knowledge that men, even doctors, had had quite such an intimate view of her while she was unconscious. She was desperately sleepy. There were visitors at the bedside. She roused herself enough to recognise her mother's face and to hear her father and Bob discussing the prospects for Wimbledon before she drifted off again.

Suddenly, it was morning. Things hurt a little bit less and she was so hungry that she could have eaten her pillow and asked for more. Breakfast was inadequate but almost wickedly enjoyable. While she ate she was oblivious of her discomfort, but the act did not last very long.

Only seconds seemed to have passed, but the day had moved on. The medical miscellany came round. Jenny was examined by the surgeon, praised by the doctor and exhibited to students. When they moved on, the doctor lingered. "If all goes well, you can go home in two or three days."

"Why not now?"

"We want to see that your graft's taking. And I wouldn't want you using that wrist more than necessary. You yourself wouldn't want to flex it. Do you have anyone to look after you?"

Jenny had not given much thought to where she would go to recuperate. Her flat was presumably uninhabitable and, although her family would doubtless squeeze up and make space for her again, she suspected that her old room had already become a valued part of their *Lebensraum*. Besides, her mother would drive her mad with fussing and her father would ease her in the direction of university and put every obstacle in the way of a resumption of her new career. She had escaped once, but she might never escape again. She admitted that aftercare might be a problem. In the privacy of her mind she added, *They'll never take me alive.*

The doctor noticed her faint smile and thought how plucky she was. "Then relax," he said, "and think yourself lucky that for once we're not short of beds. Otherwise you'd probably be standing at the bus stop with your suitcase by now." He winked to show that he was joking and moved on to catch up with the team.

The anaesthetist visited her to tell her the punchline

to his joke. Jenny laughed politely although she had forgotten how it began.

Jenny pushed her problem aside as being much too difficult to solve in her woozy state. She dozed again. Lunch was almost as welcome as breakfast had been. Then she had time to resume her worrying over a future which seemed increasingly uncertain.

It was almost a relief to be interrupted by visiting hour and the arrival of her parents. Mr and Mrs Ambleton had been allowed only partial knowledge of the background to the arson case and Jenny had said nothing to them about her other worries, so their conversation was stilted and limited to generalities. When Jenny mentioned the possibility of her release in two or three days' time, she was perturbed but not surprised at the confident assumption that she would return to her old home. She made a non-committal reply.

As they were about to leave, Mrs Ambleton suddenly delved in her handbag. "I spent most of yesterday going through your boxes," she said. "Such a load of junk! I'm sure you'll never want to see half of it again."

It might be junk, but it represented what might well prove to be the first quarter of Jenny's life. "Probably not," she said. "But which half?"

The question went over Mrs Ambleton's head. "I found it at last and nearly forgot it," she said. Jenny looked blank. "The passenger list you were asking for. I brought it with me." She handed over a few printed pages stapled together into a booklet.

As soon as her parents were beyond earshot, Jenny opened the passenger list with frantic fingers. The list had been prepared in the purser's office as an on-board telephone directory, but the telephone numbers were the same as the cabin numbers.

Mr and Mrs Oliver were listed in Cabin 238.

Jenny began to get out of bed but as soon as she tried to stand she found that her head was swimming. Her friend the nurse passed by, turned back and hurried in. "You get up tomorrow," she said, "with me to help you. Today, you stay in bed."

"Well, all right," Jenny said. "Can you bring me the plug-in telephone trolley?"

"This room doesn't have a socket for it."

Jenny kept her temper. "Then will you phone my agent and tell him to come and see me, quick?" The nurse hesitated. "Or I'll tell sister you were smoking in here."

"You wouldn't really," said the nurse uncertainly. "But I'll call him for you anyway. Give me the number."

To Jenny's disappointment Bob did not make an appearance that afternoon, but he was the first visitor in the evening. Jenny decided that they must have established a telepathic rapport, because instead of flowers he had brought a large box of chocolates. Jenny, still ravenous after her long starvation, remembered to offer them to him before falling on them greedily.

He asked how she was doing after the operation.

"Hungry and sore," she said. "They say I'll get out in two or three days, probably. That's if I'm good and if the graft takes and if they need the bed and if pigs fly. After that, instead of living out of my cardboard cartons I'll probably be living *in* one. But never mind that. Take a look at this passenger list."

Gerald Hammond

Bob looked and raised his eyebrows. "This looks good," he said. "We've been hoping for real evidence that he was cheating his wife. When it comes to motive, that's one of the strongest. Cabin two-three-eight." He jotted the number in the notebook which was his ever-present companion. "I'll check it out and get it verified by the company."

"And let me know? I've got to get this embargo lifted and start earning some money soon."

"I'll keep you posted." He reached out and patted her hand and then, as if unaware, retained hold of it. "But don't go fretting yourself. You can't start rushing around and taking photographs just yet. Things will work out. Trust me, I know what I'm talking about." He released her hand and took a paper out of his briefcase. "Fill in the rest of this claim form. Or if you don't feel up to writing I'll fill it in for you."

Jenny took the form. Much of it was already completed in a meticulous script. "Where did you get the figure for repair and redecoration?" she asked.

"From a firm just up the road. The boss owes me a favour – I pinned down an employee who was knocking off his materials and selling them cheap to his rivals – so he hurried the estimate. You'll have to tell me what you paid for the developing and printing equipment and your computer."

Jenny quoted them from memory. "But the receipts have gone up in smoke," she said. "I can verify them from my bank statement if they don't believe me. The figure you've put on my bed and the sitting-room suite looks a bit hefty," she said.

"I'd be the last person to suggest ripping off an

130

insurance company," Bob said with a perfectly straight face. "That would be against the law which I've sworn to uphold. But I decided that you deserved something of quality, new for old, after the way *they've* tried to rip *you* off. I went to see the branch manager. That was the man who came to see you, by the way. He didn't impress me, except as a highly trained but untrustworthy nonentity.

"I thought at first that he was just trying to make his figures look good, or was afraid of getting a rap over the knuckles for accepting a claim on a policy only a couple of days old. But he was so tense and overemphatic that I'm sure that it was conscience making a coward of him. I think he's afraid of being suspected of setting up a racket – selling a policy to a confederate and arranging a claim on it before the ink was dry. I told him that I was a police officer investigating the cases of arson and that you were working for the police as a civilian employee. I added that I was just behind you when the fire started.

"He was a bit sniffy, so much so that I think that he may already have that suspicion hanging over his head. I insisted on phoning his head office in his presence and speaking to the general manager. You see, I know that the firm's very jealous of its reputation for fair dealing. I spelled out the same facts and then read him your letter and the receipt. He said that he'd look into it."

"That doesn't sound very hopeful. That's what they always say when they don't intend to do a damn thing."

"It's all that you could expect from a voice on the phone. He'll be phoning my superiors for verification."

"Will he get it?"

Bob smiled grimly. "No doubt of that. I showed the papers to DI Largs and he was furious. His sense of right and wrong and his absolute certainty that he alone knows which is which make him a pain in the backside to his loyal and intelligent subordinates such as myself, but they're also what make him a good policeman. He wanted to arrest your Mr J. Asquith for fraud until I pointed out that the attempt to return your money knocked that on the head. Did I tell you that he subscribes to an orphanage in Albania?"

"No, you didn't." Jenny was smitten with sudden insight. "And you didn't say that you also make donations to it."

Bob's almost imperceptible jump was enough to tell her that she had hit the nail on the head. But, "What makes you think that?" he said.

"Something in your voice. And it would explain why you're the apple of his eye."

"I'm not," Bob protested. "And if I was, it could be because I'm what I said, loyal and intelligent. And if I did, it wouldn't be because I wanted to be the apple of his eye, wherever that extraordinary expression comes from."

"I know that," Jenny said.

They wasted a few minutes in debating what apples had to do with eyes and why the combination should be favoured before returning to business. The claim form was accompanied by a note on paper with the police letterhead, describing the fire and certifying that Miss Ambleton, so far from starting the fire, had been of help towards catching the serial arsonist. It was signed by DI Largs.

Jenny's spirits lifted. Between them, they filled in the blanks in the claim form. Bob returned it to his briefcase and took out several brightly coloured catalogues. "You know the big furniture store, Galbraith's?" he asked. "But of course you do. I based the prices in the claim form on these. Let me know your choices, including colours, so that I can get orders placed."

"But—" Jenny began.

"When the time comes, of course. Are you still of the same mind about your colour schemes?"

"Yes. But, Bob, dear Bob, you haven't been *listening*. I can't *afford* to have orders placed. I don't have any *money*. Hasn't that got through to you? The cupboard is bare. I know you've been terribly helpful and I'll be grateful until my dying day, but it's wasted effort." An awful suspicion occurred to her. "My father didn't put you up to this, did he? He isn't sticking his financial oar in?"

Bob looked at her solemnly. "The place has to be repaired some time. Do you want my help or don't you?"

"Yes, of course I do. I don't know what I'd do if I didn't have it. It's just—"

"And what about curtains?"

"I don't believe this. Bob, I didn't even *have* curtains."

"You'll have to get some unless you want to become known as the Poor Man's Television. By the time I'm through with them, Norfolk General will be delighted to buy you curtains. So trust me. Unless you'd like to go back to living at home until the insurance kicks through and while the work gets done?"

"Ouch!" She sighed. "There's nothing I'd like less. It's taken me all my life to flee the nest. But I think I'm going to have to. And I still hate taking up so much of your time. I want you to be concentrating on the arson investigation."

"I'm pulling my weight, believe me."

Jenny half-closed her eyes and regarded him doubtfully. "How is it going? Or aren't you allowed to say?"

He smiled. "You know so much already that a little more won't do any harm. And I have your promise, so I trust your discretion. It's a matter of backtracking. Nobody can do anything without leaving some sort of a trail behind them, if you can only find it. Contact traces. Tiny signals in people's memories. Times when they weren't where they were supposed to be. That sort of thing. And, of course, photographic images where a busybody photographer happened to catch them."

She felt a pleasant sense of being useful – a member, albeit peripheral, of the team. "Are my photographs helping, then?"

"It's too early to be certain. We have people going through your enlargements, but the faces are very small so when they come across possible repeats the negatives get sent for those faces to be pulled up larger. That means a delay and when we get them back they usually turn out to be different people. Or probably different people – we lose definition and computer enhancement is an uncertain business. So we end up with some possibles and you'd be amazed how many stout women with white hair there are in the world."

"What about thin women with their hair tinted sort of auburn?"

"Plenty of thin women. Hair colour isn't very reliable by night in the light of an electronic flash."

"I let you down, then?"

"Not a bit of it. Considering the conditions, general opinion is that you worked wonders. It's just that we may be asking too much of shots taken in a poor light and only intended to illustrate the general ghoulishness of people who gather to see other people's property go up in flames. That was what you were after?"

"That's it exactly," she said. "Very perceptive of you. That and some nice dramatic low-key, available-light shots for my finals exhibition."

"Then again, and switching back to what's probably a different series of attacks, we know that whoever fired the Oliver house and your flat had access to sodium chlorate. Mrs Morrissey has confirmed chlorate, by the way, and traces of sugar. Having a suspect ought to be a help, but we've tried Oliver's car for chlorate and they've identified traces of every chemical used in plant propagation and weedkilling, which in view of his business is unsurprising."

"How did he react to having his car searched?" Jenny asked.

"His car and his office and his outbuildings. Much as you'd expect in the circumstances. Innocent indignation. He fulminated against you, by the way, but I wouldn't let it worry you. Sticks and stones, yes. Words, no. We've interviewed him twice. He acts as though he's being very open and honest with us, but he won't say who was his lady-friend. The real Mrs Oliver's doctor confirms that her migraine prescription would undoubtedly put her to sleep. We have other lines of enquiry. For instance, somebody had to enter your flat between the time that we went out, just after ten, and the time that we returned."

"An hour or so before we came back," Jenny said. "There had to be time for the ammonium iodide to dry."

"Good point." Bob made a note. "But of course you'd know about that. Where were you at school? They're probably still looking for the mad bomber."

"I don't think I'll tell you that, in case they really are."

"Sensible of you, but your mother will tell me – she enjoys regaling me with details of your early life. I've heard all about the time you were caught stealing apples and she's promised to show me a photograph of you when you were a pixie in the school play."

"I'll never speak to either of you again if she does!"

"She will and you will. We're looking for witnesses who saw a visitor. Hundreds of people seemed to have entered our building and we have to eliminate each of them as best we can. Also, assuming that your guess was good, somebody had to buy crystals of iodine; not a common purchase these days – iodine has been replaced by more sophisticated antiseptics. We're trying the chemist's shops on the routes between Mr Oliver's house, his business and the two places where his staff are carrying out landscaping contracts. There have been several sales – so far, all to boys who can be presumed to want it for the same trick that you used to pull. We'll have to warn the schools."

"Spoilsport!" Jenny said.

"Yes. Of course, somebody may have persuaded a boy

to make the purchase for them, so again we have to try to trace and eliminate. It all takes manpower, which is a commodity in short supply these days."

"Especially if one of the most highly thought-of young officers is spending all his time in here."

Bob picked up one of the catalogues. He appeared to be studying it but he held it so that Jenny could see a picture of a very upmarket suite of settee and chairs. She was amused to see that she had embarrassed him. "This is Sunday," he said, "and I'm on my own time. Who ever said that I was highly thought of, or the apple of anybody's eye?" he demanded.

"I did."

"But who's supposed to think highly of me?"

Jenny decided that the approval of his superiors was rightly being kept secret from Bob. "I do," she said. "You're a pal."

He made his escape shortly afterwards, leaving Jenny to an abstracted study of his catalogues.

* * *

He returned the following afternoon. Jenny, in the meantime, had had little to do but think and she had tried to confine her thinking to the subject of arson. "What about the boy who tried to break into my car?" she asked. "Does he show up in any of the photographs?"

"We think so, but we're not sure. I only caught a glimpse of him. There are one or two vague faces, half-hidden and badly lit, which might be his. But they could belong to any skinny youth, or even a girl. We may be being deluded by a windcheater of common design."

"You'd better let me see the photographs. I might know him again. What else has been going on?"

"We're still following the lines that I told you about yesterday. Have you made a choice of furniture yet?"

Jenny sighed. "I've marked my favourites, and the colours I'll get them in when my lottery ticket hits the jackpot or Norfolk General coughs up, whichever comes first, but I really can't put my mind to that sort of expenditure while I've got financial disaster hanging over me. Has the big panjandrum at Norfolk General been back in touch yet?"

"Not yet, but he will," Bob said firmly. "Did I tell you that I said that you were on the point of showing the letter and receipt to the consumer affairs programmes? That shook him up more than somewhat."

"You could tell that over the phone?"

"Certainly. I heard him break wind."

He sounded perfectly serious but Jenny looked at him closely and saw that he was hiding a mischievous smile. It struck her that their conversation was being led around in circles carefully chosen to distract her. "There's something you're not telling me," she said. "What is it?"

"Am I as easy to read as that?" he asked ruefully. "Maybe I'm in the wrong job. Detectives are supposed to remain inscrutable. It's the little matter of what we assume to be Mr Oliver's motive."

"It's bad news, isn't it?"

"Possibly. Call it a lack of good news. We followed up that passenger list with the shipping company. The Mr and Mrs Oliver in Cabin Two-three-eight are an elderly couple from Harrogate who've sailed with them many times before."

Jernny was about to clutch her brow but she remembered in time that her brow was too sensitive to be clutched. "Oh Lord!" she said. "That will really sink us with the lawyers. Is it all right if I break the news to my agent?"

"I don't see why not. The papers will be finding out for themselves any time now and I should think he'll be the next to know about it."

Bob had to hurry away to attend a briefing meeting. She could hardly blame him for doing his job but all the same she felt deserted. She chewed her lip until Dan Mandible, responding to her summons, arrived shortly before the end of visiting hours. He enquired politely after her recovery but she could see that his mind wasn't taking in her replies. She produced the passenger list. "I wanted to show you this," she said, "but—"

He was too quick, almost snatching it from her. It was already open at the O's. "But this is just what we need," he said. "Mr and Mrs. Wait till I show this to those editors."

"I'm sorry," she said. "But the police have already been in touch with the cruise line. These Olivers are an elderly couple from Harrogate or somewhere, well known to the crew."

Dan made a sound of distress and she cursed herself for clumsily raising his hopes. At the same moment another thought struck her. "But if these are the wrong Olivers," she said, "our Mr Oliver must have sailed under some other name. What would he do about passports?"

Dan's face lost some of the look of a bloodhound about to be put down. His eyes began to smile again. "Passports are easy," he said. "When I was a reporter, I had a dozen of them in different names. Sometimes a quiet flit out of some turbulent area seemed called for."

"I must call the police. Or would you do it for me? Tell them—"

"The police certainly won't have missed that point," Dan said. She watched his body language as he relaxed. "And they'll have the published copies of your photograph to work from. All the same, with manpower as it is, it's going to take them an age to find out what name the couple were using. That's the kind of thing an investigative journalist can do better and quicker – and when he's got it for them they're far more likely to publish and be damned and claim the credit for the discovery than if they'd got it off the police. That would let us right off the hook. I'll have a word in the friendlier editors' ears. I know just the man. He didn't publish the original photograph, so he'll be delighted to hold the others up to ridicule."

The weather had turned fine. She could see children playing in the hospital garden, which looked much more floriferous, more colourful, more generally attractive than before. She was sure that just outside her range of vision would be picturesque wonders, feats of heroism, human suffering, hilarious comedy, all screaming to be captured by her camera. She developed an attack of the fidgets when, for some reason which nobody ever explained to her satisfactorily, her stay was extended by another day. Even her friend the nurse was driven to tell her, quite kindly, to shut up and stop grizzling. But on the Wednesday she was told at last that she could definitely go home on the morrow.

140

Jenny was now walking, fairly steadily, around the wards. Bob Welles, when he visited her that evening, remarked, "You don't seem pleased to be getting out." Another chair had been borrowed and they were sitting at the window like an ordinary couple.

"I shan't be sorry to leave this haunt of hygiene, bedpans and boredom," Jenny said. "I just wish that I could afford to go to a hotel, or abroad, or anywhere." She noticed that he was wearing a tie for the first time during their acquaintance. It was not a very beautiful tie, but it was a gesture. She made up her mind to buy him a better tie, just as a gesture of gratitude and between friends.

"I'm not too happy about you going back to your old home," Bob said, "but for a different reason. You're the one person who has seen certain faces and the only one we've met so far who can testify to the fact that Mr Oliver introduced a woman to you as his wife who definitely wasn't, unless he's a bigamist. What's more, God knows what little treasures – like that passenger list – may still linger, or be thought to linger, among your odds and ends. I've been told to look after you. In here, I could be fairly sure that you were safe – it isn't as easy in practice to sneak into a hospital and do somebody a mischief as the TV writers would have you believe. Hospital staff tend to know each other and the properly authorised visitors. We tipped them off to look twice at anyone in a surgeon's mask, to watch your doorway during visiting hours and to call security if anyone behaves even more oddly than the average hospital visitor. In your old home, and probably alone for most of the day, you could be vulnerable. And I don't suppose that your parents would take kindly to the attentions of an arsonist."

"I don't suppose they would. But if this is leading up to a suggestion that I stay in here indefinitely, dream on! Or are you thinking along the lines of protective custody?"

His face creased in amusement. "You could put it that way, I suppose. I was going to offer you the use of my spare bedroom. Unconventional, perhaps, but the conventions don't count the way they used to. At least you'd be on the spot to oversee the refurbishment of your flat."

Jenny felt a momentary upwelling of relief. Instead of her old home, and relationships haunted by memories of a happy enough childhood but one which she was habituated to think of as oppressive, she was being offered freedom and the companionship of a friendly and, she had to admit, rather dishy young man. In a few seconds, her spirits fell again. "I love the idea," she said, "and I'm terribly grateful, but can you imagine what my mother would say?"

"You care what your mother says? Or thinks?"

Jenny had to stop and consider. "I suppose I do," she said. "Reason tells me that her opinions are no longer binding on me, but some deeply ingrained habit left over from my early childhood insists that she's going to put me over her knee and smack my bottom."

"We could at least give her the chance to say what she has to say."

"You just want to see me getting my bottom smacked."

"There is that, of course," Bob agreed.

Flamescape

"At the very, very least, she'll suspect you of moon-lighting as a white slaver."

"I should make that sort of money," Bob said.

Mrs Ambleton, when she arrived, flabbergasted her daughter by raising no more than the most feeble objections to the plan. "After all," she said at last, "I wouldn't expect a sensible young policeman to behave with anything less than perfect propriety towards a teenage witness. He'd surely be risking his whole career."

Jenny, who usually managed to think of herself as being very nearly twenty and resented being referred to as a teenager, was piqued at being so unwanted and yet she was greatly relieved.

Her usual workaday garments had suffered from fire, water and in places from being slit for easier removal and had been scrapped. Her underwear, although definitely the worse for its experiences, was considered salvable. Jenny had asked her mother to bring her a selection from those clothes which had been awaiting transfer to the flat, in particular her oldest pair of jeans, now uncomfortably tight and fashionably disintegrating, as being suitable for making a start to cleaning out the flat and scrubbing the soot off all surfaces. Instead, she found herself primly dressed in a girlish summer frock which her mother had purchased for the occasion, together with a pair of smart shoes which Jenny considered intolerably uncomfortable. Mrs Ambleton had even added a new pair of very thin tights.

Jenny's father was away on business and her mother was occupied with one of her many committees, so Bob Welles had volunteered to collect Jenny from the hospital. She was waiting patiently, nursing a carrier bag

143

which held what had been the contents of her pockets at the time of the fire, when he walked in. He looked at her in mild surprise.

Jenny felt suddenly shy. "You've seen me before," she said gruffly.

"I've seen a tomboy before," Bob said. "Now I see a young lady. You look good enough to take to a garden party. I can hardly see the dressings and the bandage could pass for a headband."

"Bah!" Jenny said. But she caught herself smiling.

Bob had brought his own car, a two-year-old Vauxhall of deliberately shabby appearance. He spent the journey explaining to Jenny that a better or shinier car might attract just the sort of attention that he should avoid. He repeated himself more than once. Jenny decided that he was nervous and wondered what on earth he could find to be nervous about. He had shown no sign of being shy with girls. Perhaps there was a woman staying in his flat and he was wondering how she would take the revelation. She wondered the same thing.

They called at the police garage to collect her jeep. Jenny attracted a whistle from one of the mechanics. The act of driving had become unfamiliar and she found that she was having to pre-plan every action as though she were a learner-driver again. They drew up outside the flats and parked in adjacent slots. "My windows are open," Jenny said.

"I left them that way to let the smell dissipate. Come on in."

The hall seemed undamaged except that her flat had a new door. She waited to be shown to his spare room, but Bob said, "Come and take a look at your flat."

She sighed. "I suppose I'll have to face up to it some time."

He nodded and dug a hand into his pocket. "You'll need these keys. You have security locks now, not just a cheap night-latch that any fool could and did open with a piece of plastic." He showed her the way of the locks and then stood back.

Jenny opened the door.

She stepped back to read the number but it really was her flat.

"What . . . ?" she said. "What . . . ?"

"Come and sit down," he said. He was grinning all over his face, she thought, right up over his head and probably half-way down his back. He led her to a chair in her own sitting room and took the seat opposite her. "Your morale was rather low, so your parents and I organised it between us."

"But I can't pay for all this," she said helplessly. The suite was straight out of the catalogue and she remembered the price. The new carpet must have cost the same as its predecessor. The walls and woodwork had been repainted the colours of her choice. The lingering smell of paint was barely perceptible.

"I jumped the gun, just a little," Bob said, "but whenever your insurers began to quibble at what really is rather a formidable total I threatened to give the story and the documents to *Watchdog*. So they came and looked and I got a verbal nod over the phone. We're still haggling over the value of your clothes, but otherwise they seem to be coming round."

"I'm not surprised if they're jibbing a bit," Jenny said. "You talked me into quoting figures a film star might have boggled at." There were harmonising curtains, she saw, which had been drawn back so that they could not spoil the surprise by being seen from outside.

"It'll cost you most of that to replace your wardrobe," Bob said airily. "Anything left over, think of as damages for giving you a bad time at the start. The furniture's on sale-or-return. If the insurance money won't cover it and you don't get your fees for the photographs, you'll have to put it back or start a hire purchase. Regarding computer and photographic gear, the money's coming but you'll have to do your own shopping."

"That's my mother's coffee table," she said weakly.

"Her second-best coffee table, she tells me. It's on semi-permanent loan. She went to a jumble sale and got you some pans and dishes and so on. She had been letting you make your own way because that was what you seemed to want, but when you needed her she was there for you."

Jenny was still looking around, stunned. Her colours chosen for the sitting room had come as a shock at first, but as she became used to them they began to look better and better. A pale blue, contrasted with the hue of copper-beech leaves in autumn, was repeated in the carpet and fabrics with some touches of golden yellow. There were some almost-harmonising water-colours on the walls. "You've all been to so much trouble," she said.

"If it's made you happy . . ."

"Oh, it has!" Jenny felt tears coming.

"If you're really happy, turn off the waterworks." Not for the first time, he lent her a handkerchief.

"I'm happy," she said, wiping her eyes and laughing. "And the pictures? Where did they come from?"

146

"One's from the same jumble sale. One's mine, on loan. And your brother bought you the third one. It's your present for Christmas and your next birthday combined."

Jenny jumped up and walked around looking at things. The flat was still rather bare. She liked it that way, but no doubt the clutter which usually surrounded her would soon make a return. "Well," she said at last, "I must say I'm stunned. It looks absolutely marvellous and I can't thank you all enough. I must get hold of Mum and tell her how much I appreciate it. I didn't think I'd get it as good as this for about a thousand years. I'm dumbstruck. I'm speechless."

"If this is speechless," Bob said, "I hope I'm not there when you find your voice."

"Don't be sarky. I'll have to give you all a dinner party when I'm organised. For the moment, give me time to do a little shopping and I'll make us both some lunch."

"You're on! But there's no hurry. I'll go and clock on again at the factory and I'll be back at – what shall we say? – one o'clock?"

"Let's say just that," Jenny said happily. She blew her nose. "You'll get this back when I've laundered it."

In the tiny kitchen, the cooker and fridge-freezer were new. More hire purchase, she supposed, if the insurance money failed to arrive. In a hundred years or so, it would all be hers.

Jenny had no dining furniture yet, but she refused to serve lunch in Bob's flat. This, she explained to him on his return, was by way of being a preliminary house-warming party. So they took soup from mugs, ate quiche from plates on their knees and finished with fresh fruit and coffee.

As they finished, Bob said, "I'd like your help this evening. Could you be ready to go out at about six? And will you be strong enough for an outing?"

"Yes, of course. When will you hear back from the cruise line?"

"We've had a result just now. We sent the picture by radio and the purser recognised them. Mr Oliver and his lady-friend travelled as Mr and Mrs Cromwell. Easy to remember, I suppose – Oliver, Cromwell. Are you going to take legal advice?"

Jenny admitted that she was still nervous about the threat of a libel action, but not nervous enough yet to commit money to solicitor's fees.

"I think perhaps you should," Bob said, "if only to feel that you're doing something instead of sitting around and waiting for it to fall on you."

"Nothing's changed," Jenny said. "I still don't have any money. And I don't think that you can get Legal Aid in a libel case."

"But you wouldn't be defending the libel case, that would be for the papers. If you can feed them the right information, they may be persuaded to fight." He paused.

Something in his attitude alerted Jenny. "There's more, isn't there?" she said.

"There you go again, reading my mind. I don't want to worry you."

"Go ahead and worry me. Perhaps it's time I was worried. While I was in hospital you were sheltering me and I was grateful. Now it's time that I faced realities." She braced herself.

Bob nodded appreciatively. "You're a girl with guts. But you have to guard your back against being made the scapegoat by the papers if they lose out. That's why I think you need legal advice."

Jenny stood up and lifted the crockery from the coffee table, but instead of carrying it through to the little kitchen she stopped in front of Bob and said, "I don't understand. The photograph shows them together. They were travelling as a married couple. If he has another woman in his life and wants to marry her, surely that gives him a motive for killing his wife?"

"Not necessarily," Bob said slowly. "He may not be guilty of anything worse than having a fling while his wife was abroad. Remember, motive never makes a case. Everybody has motivation to commit crimes but comparatively few actually give in to temptation. Mr Oliver admits to having had a mad fling. Most men can succumb to temptation, he said, but he still maintains that he loved his wife and mourns her passing."

"Do you believe him?"

"As the facts come in we find fewer and fewer reasons to disbelieve him. He was told that he could see her body . . . Do you really want to hear all these grisly details?"

Jenny swallowed. "Go on," she said. "I need to know what I'm up against."

"He immediately insisted on seeing the body and his reaction wasn't that of a murderer. It was an awful sight – I had to be present during the autopsy, so I know – but he kissed the half-burnt remains and I'm told that he seemed absolutely sincere. He was producing real tears. They had to take him away and feed him a sedative.

"We've been watching him and we've been through his outbuildings and his office. We sometimes get cases of arson where the culprit has burnt his own premises, either to defraud his insurers or to cover up some other crime. One of the things that we watch out for is that, in almost all such cases, the arsonist has removed property of real or sentimental value to somewhere safe. We've found nothing of that sort. Mr Oliver seems to have lost some valuable antiques, all his clothes other than what he was wearing at the time and all his personal papers. In fact, he's having the devil's own job reconstructing the figures for his overdue tax return."

"In other words, he may not be guilty?"

"It's too early to say. I just want you to be aware of the possibility and to realise that if he really is innocent – at least in the eyes of the law – it may be argued that your production of the photograph caused him great embarrassment. As I said before, I don't think that it will come to that but you should be ready. If he's been badly hurt, he may be looking for somebody to lash out at and you may be a softer target than the papers. He's already got his apology and retraction out of them. A good lawyer might be able to argue him out of taking it any further."

Jenny decided that there would be no profit just yet in fretting about future dangers. There was a more immediate question in her mind. She carried the crockery into the kitchen and came back. "Do you agree with him?" she asked. "This is important."

"About what?"

"About most men succumbing to temptation to cheat on their wives?"

Bob laughed and got to his feet. "Ask me again in about ten years or when I have a wife of my own," he said. "Whichever comes first."

Jenny opened her mouth to ask another question but closed it without speaking.

Eight

Jenny found that her first day out of hospital was exhausting her. She lay down on her new bed and dozed for a few minutes, but exhilaration and worry between them kept her awake. She spent what was left of the afternoon gloating over her flat in its new guise, rearranging the furniture and stocking the refrigerator from the nearby shops using the money earned from the police. She snacked on the remains of the quiche and was waiting at the door when Bob returned at six. It had become a dark and damp evening and she had expended a few of her remaining pounds on a nylon mackintosh to keep her only good dress dry. She contemplated replacing her ruined umbrella, but umbrellas were expensive and she decided that food came first.

She had reclaimed her cameras from Bob's flat and he looked at her in amusement when she lugged the heavy case out to him. He made as if to put it in the boot but she stopped him. "On the back seat," she said, "where I can make a quick grab."

They got into the car. Bob drove off. "I don't think that you'll see flying elephants this trip," he said, "and if something interesting does turn up it'll already be on tape and I'll get you a copy. But suit yourself."

152

This was intriguing. "Where are we going, then?" she said.

"I thought you were never going to ask."

"I didn't need to know," she said simply. "I owe you so many favours that I'll do whatever you want."

Bob was silent from one traffic light to the next, apparently stunned by this *carte blanche*. When the light had changed again, he said, "We're going to the control room where they watch the security video cameras in the city centre. You're going to help the police with their enquiries."

"The police usually say that about a suspect being interrogated."

"Any interrogation will be friendly. You're the only person we know to have had a good look at the boy and at Mrs Cromwell, so called. A still photograph is never half as informative as the real thing or even a moving picture. It lacks angles and movement and a voice."

"All right," she said. "It'll keep me off the streets."

He parked in a private open car park near the cathedral and they climbed some hollow-sounding stairs. Jenny found herself in a room with a low level of light, where three uniformed officers – one elderly, one with his leg in a cast and one WPC at an advanced stage of pregnancy – were watching more than a dozen monitors. This was evidently where the unfit could still give useful service.

Bob introduced Jenny around and then gave her a chair in front of an isolated monitor. "The clips we picked out this morning," he said to the elderly man. "The ones of the boy. See if he's in any of these shots," he told Jenny.

A crowd scene came on the monitor. There was a fountain in the foreground which Jenny recognised as being in the city's major indoor shopping centre, but she had little time to scan individual faces. The scene was replaced by one of a group of youths loitering near the escalator. "I think that's the one," she said quickly. She indicated a boy who was lingering on the fringe of the group as if uncertain of his welcome.

The scene changed again, to a street at night-time. A boy's figure came out of a shop and ran off, dodging between the passers-by. "That's him," she said. "That's exactly how he ran."

"Enough," Bob said. The picture vanished. "That's just what we hoped for. If we use you to identify him in court, nobody can say that you were given a lead. You picked him out from among others each time. Now see if you can sort him out from among other customers in a security video."

This time, the camera was looking down and across a cash-desk. A short queue of customers was settling debts with cash or credit cards. Most of the faces were in full view although sometimes slightly out of focus. A dozen came and went. Jenny heard the WPC directing a mobile unit to where a pickpocket was at work. She sat up suddenly. One face leaped out at her and every feature rang its own signal in her memory. "That is definitely the one," she said.

"Then you may as well see what came a second later," said Bob. The picture vanished, the screen was blank for a few moments and then a different scene appeared. The forecourt of a filling station. It looked familiar. Jenny had bought petrol there many times. The same youth came out of the doorway. He was carrying an object the size and shape of a petrol can. This time the screen remained blank.

Bob said, "I'll get you to sign a statement to the effect that you picked him out of a series of fourteen customers on the video. That should stand up in court."

"We've got to find him first," said the elderly man – a Sergeant Forbes, Jenny remembered from the introductions.

"We'll need a little luck," Bob said, "but sometimes we can give luck a nudge in the right direction. The Fire Service is planning a controlled burning."

"What's a controlled burning?" Jenny asked.

"A building that isn't even worth pulling down. It has dry rot, wet rot, woodworm, everything but dandruff. They take out anything salvageable, like lead piping, and torch the rest with fire crews standing by. It saves the demolition contractor the cost of pulling it down and carting it away to a bonfire somewhere else. If we give it enough publicity, it should attract him and any other pyromaniacs."

"We've been watching a mile of footage," said Sergeant Forbes, "and showing it to relays of officers and nobody knows who he is—"

"*I* don't know who he is," said the pregnant WPC, "but isn't that him again?"

She was pointing to a different screen. The figure of a youth was walking along a street of shops, almost deserted so late of a dull, drizzly evening. He was hunched against the cold and damp but he turned to look behind him. At the same moment the operator zoomed closer. "Yes!" Jenny said.

"Keep the cameras on him for as long as you can," Bob snapped. "I'll try to catch up with him by car. Send a car to wait at Market Cross in case I need some help. You'd better come with me and pick him out," he threw in Jenny's direction.

They clattered down the stairs and into the car park. Bob had his car open, running and into gear before Jenny had time to do more than catch up and throw herself into the passenger seat. They shot out under the radiator of an indignant bus while Jenny was still trying to fasten her seat-belt. Although Bob's car was private and unmarked, Jenny had half expected him to slap a blue light on the roof and switch on a klaxon, but she was disappointed. Another example of overexposure to American television, she thought.

A left turn, a right, a descent down a steep hill. The rain had stopped and there was a streak of belated brightness in the sky, but people seemed to have given up and gone home. The tarmac was still wet and the car tended to slide. They slewed into a small square lined with shops. "That was the camera up there," Bob said, pointing. "He must have gone this way." He had a personal radio in one hand. He gave an identification and asked to be connected to the CCTV room. Sergeant Forbes had no news for him.

They were in an area strange to Jenny. She tried to look up the side streets as they passed them. "Somebody there," she said suddenly. "Small and thin. Could have been him."

"If he's still on foot, I don't think that he could have come this far," Bob said. He used the next junction to spin the car and whisked them back. The figure that Jenny had seen was a hundred yards up the side street. When they overtook it, it turned out to be female, red-haired and meeting its boyfriend on the doorstep of a small pub.

"Lost him," Bob said.

"Sorry."

"Not your fault. You did the right thing. It just turned out to be the wrong person."

Sergeant Forbes's voice, tinny and distorted, came out of the radio. "He just crossed the bottom of Clarion Street, or somebody very like him."

"Ha!" Bob jerked the car round and booted it up a side street. "Has a car reached Market Cross yet?"

"Yes."

"Have them move to Southeby Street and warn us if a thin youth with a loose coat goes by."

They doubled back and looped around old streets, a mixture of pre-Planning Act commercial-industrial and low-cost housing. Jenny had not realised that her city had such an under-belly but Bob seemed to be familiar with every alleyway. She would have to come back and prowl with a camera. More people were out and about, now that the rain was staying off. Several more false alarms necessitated backtracking. Bob started circling a roundabout, his eyes darting along the five radiating streets. It was half an hour since the last sighting.

"Hopeless," he said at last. "Or . . . maybe it isn't." He lifted the radio. "Fire," he said. "Where is it?"

Jenny looked and saw a puff of smoke above the rooftops.

They were in an area of poor reception. The radio chattered a few words in which the consonants were inaudible, but Bob seemed to understand. "Tell the car to stay at Southeby Street until I call for them," he told the radio. "I don't want him spooked and running again." He left the roundabout and bustled the car round a corner and over a main road.

Jenny turned in her seat, unlocked her camera case and took out the faithful Pentax. The standard lens was already fitted. The light was fading again so she added the flash unit. The road was rough and she had to fumble with the plug. When she looked up they were traversing a neglected street between abandoned buildings.

Two fire appliances had beaten them to what had once been a church and church hall. A third appliance was behind them and Bob swung out of the way. Soft pillows of smoke were rising above the buildings and flames were flowering out of broken windows. The buildings were hemmed in by others, equally old but still in commercial use, and the firefighters were struggling to prevent the flames from spreading. Jenny could hear at least one fire alarm shrilling above all other sounds. A fourth fire appliance arrived.

Bob was out of the car, walking swiftly away and scanning faces. Jenny would have followed but she was not going to leave the rest of her camera equipment for the first passing thief to make off with. Bob seemed to have vanished, taking the key with him. She locked the car manually. Out of habit, she occupied a minute or two in taking shots of the fire and of the bystanders who were already gathering and getting in the firefighters' way.

The burning buildings were fronted by an open space of apparently derelict ground. She had worked her way round to the further end, stumbling over the uneven surface and trying not to splash through puddles in her unsuitable shoes, when she saw Bob returning. He was holding one cuff of a pair of handcuffs, the other end being round the right wrist of a youth whom she had no difficulty recognising as the one who had tried to enter her car and who figured in the various photographs and videos. He was maintaining a constant moan that he "hadn't done nothing", between arguing that he was as entitled as anyone else to stay and watch the flames.

She fell in behind them as they passed her. The youth was holding his left arm stiffly to his side, as though he was injured or hiding something under his thin raincoat. There might be a need later for evidence. Or perhaps he was about to produce a weapon. Prior to calling out a warning, she raised her camera. At that moment, Bob and the boy were threading a way through a dump of abandoned household detritus. As she pressed the button the boy moved his arm and the camera flash caught an object hitting the ground. When she reached the spot she found, lying between some empty tins and an old mattress, a rubber hot-water bottle. It might easily have been mistaken for yet another item of rubbish, discarded and forgotten. Bob had noticed nothing. She picked it up by means of a twig through the moulded handle and followed on.

Captor and prisoner reached the car. "Your name?" Bob asked.

"That's for me to know an' you to find out," the youth said with a show of bravado. Close up, he was seen to be very spotty. He had a loose mouth and watery eyes.

"And find out I will," Bob said grimly. He tugged fruitlessly at the door-handle.

Jenny came up behind. She paused to take a close-up

of the boy. His sharp features suggested a primitive guile but his eyes were shifty.

"You forgot to lock the car," she told Bob. "I wasn't going to leave my other cameras to be nicked."

Bob looked up at the glowering heavens and uttered what might have been a truncated moan as a substitute for something more deeply satisfying. "Locally," he said at last very gently, "if we're at an incident and we're not going out of sight of the car and especially if we expect to come back with a prisoner, we don't lock the car. Too much time can be lost in fishing for the key and fumbling with the lock. The convention is, we drop the keys under one of the front seats. That way, somebody else can collect it or move it out of the way if they need to."

Jenny could see what came next. "And you don't have a spare key?"

"Not on me, no."

"Well, I'm sorry," Jenny said. "But I didn't know that. What about your radio? Or surely there'll be another police car here in a minute. You could call up the one from Southeby Street. They could let you in, couldn't they?"

"I can do without being let into my own car by some goon from Traffic grinning all over his face," Bob said grimly. "I'd never hear the last of it."

"Or the Fire Brigade?"

"They'd want to cut the roof off it."

The youth, who had fallen silent, seemed to find the exchange consoling. He grinned, showing uneven teeth, and suddenly found his voice. "I can let you in," he said. "If I do, will you let me go? You got no evidence."

"We've got photographs—" Bob began.

"We've got this," Jenny said, holding out the hot-water bottle. It stank of petrol. Bob said "Ha!", took it and laid it on the roof of the car.

"I never seen that before," squeaked the youth.

"I photographed you dropping it," said Jenny. "And," she added to Bob, "I reserve the right to reproduce the photograph."

"Did you really?" the youth asked. "Straight up?"

"Straight up. Didn't you see the flash? And the bag will have your fingerprints all over the smooth side."

The youth thought it over. He must have decided that Jenny was trustworthy and the jig was up. "Yeah, I saw the flash. Thought it was lightning, didn't I? All right, then," he said glumly. "The rain's coming on again an' I'm not standing here to be gawped at. Give us yer pen-knife. I won't do nothin' else with it," he added. "I'm not the violent type, to cut you up."

"You're a qualified lock-picker as well, are you?" Bob asked.

The boy shrugged. "I learn things. I'm not stupid. And I'll need a piece of wire."

"I just trod on a piece," Jenny said. She went to look for it. The blaze had a good hold of the old timbers. The water hosing onto it seemed to have little effect but at least the firefighters were managing to save the buildings on either side, for what little they were worth. The rain was still too light to do more than form a mist in the air which gave every flicker of flame its own halo. The crowd was growing but facing the flames, away from the car, unaware of the drama behind them. Behind her, she

161

could hear the youth objecting that he wanted to stay and spectate.

"That was your mistake," Bob said, "sticking around and appearing in photographs at every fire you started."

"I didn't start them," the youth said hopefully. "I just like to watch."

"How did you get to every one of them seconds after it started? We've got your hot-water bottle, remember. And we had a good look at you at the fire where Mrs Oliver died."

This time, Bob got a strong reaction. "'Ere, you can't stick me with that," the youth cried. "I just 'appened to be on a bus when I saw the smoke, so I 'opped off."

Jenny had found the piece of wire. She had also found a renewed sense of indignation. "What about my flat?" she asked sternly.

He stared at her. "What about it?"

"Where did you buy the iodine?" Bob demanded.

"Dunno what you're talking about."

"We'll talk about it at the nick."

"We got to get there, first, an' out o' this bleedin' rain."

Bob attached the handcuff to the car's door-handle before surrendering his pen-knife. Jenny handed over the wire. "I don't want nobody to see this," said the youth. "It's my own secret. You turn your backs."

"What in hell are you trying to pull?" Bob demanded.

"Straight up. I don't teach nobody this trick, not even coppers. You don' know what they'd get up to." And when Bob still hesitated, he added, "All right, then. Stay out in the rain. Call up your pals."

"Do you think I was born yesterday?"

"Must've been, to enjoy standin' 'ere an' gettin' wet through."

While Bob hesitated, Jenny felt a tickle in her nose. She got a tissue out of the pocket of her plastic mac and she sneezed violently. It proved to be deciding factor.

"All right," Bob said. "But be quick." They looked away. Seconds later there was a click. When they looked back, the handcuff was gone from the door-handle and the youth was sprinting away through the puddles. Bob took off after him but there was no doubt as to which was the more fleet of foot.

Bob came back panting. "He'd make a good wing three-quarter," he gasped. "And he's still got my pen-knife and an expensive pair of cuffs. The bugger! But did he open the car?"

Jenny tried the handle. "No," she said.

Pushed beyond his limit, Bob said another rude word. "Don't you go telling your mother I used that sort of language in front of her ewe lamb," he added.

Jenny was about to deny being anybody's ewe lamb but decided that the description was probably true. "Why should you give a damn what my mother thinks?" she asked.

"I like your mother," was all the explanation that Bob would give. He used his radio to summon the car from Southeby Street.

"Bob," Jenny said, "have you had anybody watching me?"

"I would have done, if we could have spared anybody. But we couldn't. Why?"

"There was a woman. She's gone now. She seemed to be watching us and I think she took a photograph.

But the thing is, she makes me think of somebody I've seen several times recently without quite noticing, if you know what I mean."

"I know exactly what you mean. Can you describe her?"

"I wish I'd caught her on camera," Jenny said, "but I'm fairly sure I haven't. If it's always the same woman, she's medium height, large hipped and rather short in the leg so that she waddles as she walks."

"Hair?" said Bob.

"That's the problem," Jenny said. "That's why I didn't catch on earlier. I've been seeing that figure and that distinctive walk, but her clothes have been different, and her hair. I think she must have a supply of nylon wigs and keeps changing them. That makes it very difficult to guess her age. Looking back, I think that there's usually been a small grey van nearby whenever I've seen her."

"It couldn't have been Mrs Oliver-Cromwell?"

"No way!" Jenny said. "Totally different shapes. Mrs Thingy's tall and skinny. This one's at least half a head shorter but weighs about the same, maybe more."

"Well," Bob said, "I'll ask around, but it doesn't sound like one of ours. If you see her again, call me."

Jenny slept in her new bed that night. Her mother had even equipped her with sheets and also a quilt which Jenny remembered from home. She suspected that that thrifty lady was taking advantage of the occasion to replace her older household goods while making a show of generosity by passing on the worn or outdated chattels

164

to her daughter. *Don't knock it,* Jenny told herself. She still came out on the up-side.

Her several dressings looked washable but nobody had said that she could wear them in a bath or shower and she had forgotten to ask the question. She treated herself to a sponge bath of all the bits that she could reach, dressed herself in the available clothes and had a quick breakfast.

The flat had come equipped with a telephone and the melted instrument had been replaced by one with a tapeless answering facility. (The rental, Bob had explained, would be only microscopically more than that for a bare phone.) A tiny flashing light indicated a message waiting. With some trepidation, because very little news had been good news of late, she read the labels under the buttons and pressed the right one. Dan Mandible's voice invited her to call him back. He had anticipated her anxiety and followed the request by telling her that he had a cheque for her. That addendum ensured that she would call back at once. They arranged to meet later.

The first priority was clothes. Jenny's favourites had been first to be moved to the new flat and had therefore been destroyed. She made herself as presentable as she could and set off in her jeep. Driving it was still an unfamiliar sensation which kept her mind on her driving and off her worries as she drove to her former home. The rain had blown past and the day was again bright and warm, the light too harsh for the best photography.

Her mother was, for once, in the house and Jenny, who was genuinely grateful for her refurbished and re-equipped flat, remembered to be effusive in her thanks for the many favours. These little things, she knew, were important to parents. Her mother came and chatted to her while she packed her remaining clothes into a large carton. It was not an impressive collection, being more suited to wear while gardening or doing home decoration than when appearing in public. She had been a schoolgirl and then a student, thinking of herself as strictly non-glamorous and dressing for comfort and practicality. Now that she was beginning to see herself as a female person of an age for business or even courtship, such of her wardrobe as had not been brought to the flat and burnt she would not have worn, she told herself, to be seen dead in a ditch, but when she considered it she could not think of any raiment suitable for those particular circumstances.

She borrowed an iron from her mother and pressed the damp-induced creases out of her one decent dress. She had cleaned the worst of the mud off her new and uncomfortable shoes. They had time to chat over a cup of coffee in the kitchen.

"How are you getting on with that nice Bob Welles?" Mrs Ambleton asked suddenly. "The policeman," she added, in case Jenny had forgotten. "Did he like you in that dress?"

"I think he did at first but now he's rather gone off me," Jenny said.

Her mother seemed genuinely cast down. "That's too bad!" she said. "What went wrong? You seemed to be getting on so well together."

Jenny found herself telling the story of the previous evening. As she spoke she began to see the humorous side of it and she turned it into a mildly funny story.

"Of course," she finished, "exactly what he didn't want happened and we had to be let into his car by a grinning constable from Traffic. Apparently, traffic policemen get quite used to having to let motorists into their cars so they carry a sort of flat blade to slip down the side of the window. And then we went to Bob's office or headquarters or whatever they call it—"

"The nick," her mother said wisely. "Or do they only call it that on television?"

"As a matter of fact, I've heard Bob call it that, so you're probably right. Anyway, we had to go there so that I could make a formal statement – I seem to have been doing a lot of that lately – all about having identified the boy and Bob was getting his leg pulled quite a lot. And he's gone in today to face the music. There's no escaping the fact that he had the arsonist handcuffed and let him get away and it's all my fault for locking the car."

Mrs Ambleton drew herself up. "He knew about your cameras. He should have told you the drill or even waited to lock the car himself. And he should have had his spare key on him. It seems to me that he did more things wrong that you did. And then to blame you! Just you wait until I see that young man again," she said grimly.

"I don't suppose you will see him again, except to pass in the hall when you come to visit. Anyway, I can't help wondering how a very junior policeman – he only went up to sergeant not long ago – comes to have a quite expensive flat. Do you think he takes bribes?"

"Certainly not," Mrs Ambleton said, now as indignant on Bob's behalf as she had been on her daughter's a moment earlier. "Your father went into that with his friend the superintendent. Your boyfriend got a legacy when his father died and he was given permission to buy a home. As a general rule, they don't like policemen to put down roots. A stupid policy, your father says. Every time a young policeman spots his dream house, they lose him."

"He isn't my boyfriend," Jenny said for the umpteenth time.

She had arranged to meet Dan in one of the smarter hotels. She collected her prints from the lab, parked the jeep in the hotel car park and walked in through a rear entrance. The dressing at her hairline was small enough to be covered by a traditional headband which gave her a slightly hippyish look but she still attracted one or two favourable glances from the male clientele. Even a woman with a bouffant hairdo who followed her in through the revolving doors gave her a searching glance.

Dan Mandible, also, was impressed. He swept her into the lounge for coffee and a sandwich. "You're turning into a presentable young lady," he said. "Which is all to the good, because I'm trying to get you an assignment with a fashion magazine."

"I know absolutely zip about fashion photography," Jenny told him. "We had a lecture and demonstration about it but it rather went over my head because I knew zip about fashion and cared less."

"It's a minor feature," Dan said reassuringly. "Somebody wants to break into the swimsuit market, almost as a cottage industry, so they want somebody with a good camera but no big ideas about money to photograph some models playing ball on the beach. No big deal."

"You'd better stall them for a day or two. This is the only decent dress I've got," Jenny said, "and it's too delicate for working in and it makes me look like something on a chocolate-box. Everything else that survived the fire would be barely suitable on a weekend pony-trekking."

"Then this may help." He handed her a cheque. "I persuaded the editors to pay up for the published photographs, by threatening each of them that your future scoops would go to their biggest rivals. And on Monday the *Tidings* will use your shot of the bird's nest against the background of the burning house."

"I'm not wasting this on clothes," Jenny said indignantly. "And it won't even replace my computer. But I need a mobile phone and . . . and . . ."

"You'll have to try the charity shop at the end of the street."

"I don't take charity. I'm not quite that desperate yet. Next week, perhaps, but not yet."

"They wouldn't offer you charity," Dan explained patiently. "They have given to them some very good new or nearly new clothes and they sell them for charity. I'm told that you can get some real bargains there. You've had no insurance money yet?"

"Not a groat. Bob Welles was in touch with them for me and he says that he's sure they'll pay up in the end, but I don't think that'll happen until somebody else turns out to be responsible for the fire at my flat. Which could be years, if ever."

"Much the same could be said about that libel threat."

Jenny tried not to think about the libel threat. Instead, she produced the envelope of enlargements. "Did you hear that the arsonist – not the one who did my flat, probably, but who's been starting all the other fires – was caught last night?"

"And got away. I heard. Sorry, Jenny, your news is stale."

"Thank God!" Jenny said.

"You're pleased?"

"As Punch. For my sake, not for Bob's. I've a photograph for you but I didn't want to be the one to let out the story of Bob's embarrassment." She laid an enlargement on the coffee table. "You can see the hot-water bottle just about to hit the ground. I took this as he dropped it from under his coat. The police say it's all right to use it so long as his face is blacked out."

Dan studied the picture. "Now this," he said, "I can do something with. You wouldn't care to say how the bastard managed to get away?"

"No, I wouldn't," Jenny said. "Except to say that it was all my stupid fault. And I'll put that to music and sing it, if anyone wants."

Nine

The cheque was burning a hole in Jenny's pocket. She knew that she should save it for living expenses until her troubles were sorted out, setting some aside for tax and diverting a little for the essentials that she and the flat still lacked. Instead, she crossed the street to a shop which boasted the widest range of mobile phones to be had and after a careful comparison of facilities and prices bought a compact one complete with car kit. The phone would be connected to her chosen service provider by that evening, she was promised. Although there would be a running cost to be met, the initial cost was comparatively small.

The balance of her cheque would not lend itself to shopping in the bigger stores. Dan's advice, however, had proved sound in the past and on other subjects. She looked for and found the charity shop. This proved to be a revelation. Rack upon rack of clothes greeted her, most of them seemingly brand new but in fact, the lady in charge explained, usually having been bought in expectation of a loss of weight which had not been achieved, chosen in a mad moment and discovered to be hideously unflattering when brought home, or found to have gone out of fashion during that journey.

171

Gerald Hammond

When she heard that Jenny had lost her entire wardrobe in a fire the lady, who had always wanted a daughter of her own but had only been blessed with sons, became sympathetic; and when Jenny (who until only a year or two earlier had considered it a waste of valuable partying time to pause and change clothes between helping her father in the garden and attending a friend's wedding reception) confessed that she had no idea at all what would suit her or even what looked smart or stylish, she threw herself with enthusiasm into the project. She quite understood. Jenny wanted to look good, but in clothes which would not suffer unduly if Jenny's profession took her through smoke, thorn bushes or derelict buildings, or else clothes that were cheap enough not to matter – preferably both. Quite so.

Jenny, she said, was right. The dress she was wearing was pretty but it did little for her. Jenny's black hair, red lips and pink cheeks called for something more dramatic. She would have looked well in white, but white would not be practical. Black, now . . . but Jenny had worn too much black at school and had no intention of spending her days looking like a Mediterranean widow.

But how about this well-cut trouser suit in small red and black checks, by a top designer? It had only come to the shop because the owner, who had paid a small fortune for it, found herself guided by her hostess to a settee upholstered in similar material. Or the jacket and skirt in bronze corduroy? The skirt could do with shortening by an inch or so, but in other respects each was a good fit and the colours went very well with Jenny's colouring.

The result was that Jenny spent more than she intended

but was well satisfied. The lady had a friend who undertook alterations. Jenny could pick the altered skirt up next week, but she left the shop in the trouser suit – with her dress in a Harrods carrier bag, at modest extra cost. Two doors along, she purchased a red baseball cap and, gritting her teeth at the cost, a pair of red trainers. On sudden inspiration, she offset the cost of the trainers by returning to the charity shop and selling the lady the smart but uncomfortable shoes furnished by Mrs Ambleton. From there, she made a dash to the bank to deposit Dan's cheque before any of her own could be presented.

She caught the bank just before it closed. The afternoon seemed almost to have evaporated. Bob had asked Jenny to call in during the afternoon in order to sign her statement and now, kitted out in a way that she felt to be both attractive and comfortable, she felt brave enough to face him.

As she drove, she watched the mirror for the small grey van. Almost immediately, there was one in her mirror. She pulled into a service road to let it go by. It had the name of a plumber's merchant on the side. As she set off again, another grey van passed in the opposite direction, driven by a fat man with glasses and another, similar van appeared behind her. It seemed to Jenny that the streets were suddenly full of grey vans and whether any of them, or all of them, contained Mrs Oliver-Cromwell or some other pursuer she ceased to care. She would ask Bob about it if they were still on speaking terms.

The police building was fronted by a few parking spaces for those members of the common public unlucky

enough to have business within, but those with appoint-
ments were admitted to a more generous car park beside
the police garage, entered from a side street. The gateway
was between the modern police building, a structure of
steel and glass and anodised aluminium cladding and,
on the other side of the street, a large, genuine Tudor
building, originally the town hall and magistrate's court
but now a hotel.

The guard on the gate looked carefully for Jenny's
name on a list before nodding her through. Hotel guests
had been known to usurp space in the police car park
if they could get away with it. Most of that car park
was fenced off and occupied by police cars, vehicles
stolen and recovered, tow-aways and cars being held
as evidence of one crime or another, but Jenny found a
place in a quiet corner of the accessible third. She locked
up carefully (because her cameras were in the back and
even policemen are not always quite what they used to
be) and headed for the building.

As she neared the glass doors a large figure came
blundering out, almost knocking her down. With a jolt,
she recognised the bereaved Mr Oliver. He was either
drunk or in the grip of intolerable emotion. She ducked
round him, trying to hide her face.

He might be fuddled but he was still alert. He
spun round, almost losing his balance, and swayed
forward, isolating her in a corner of brickwork. "You!"
he exclaimed.

"Good afternoon," she said politely. The car park was
remarkably empty. Here, of all places, there should have
been a dozen policemen in sight and earshot. She tried
to duck past him but he put out a hand to stop her. His

portly bulk was almost leaning against her and she could sense a fruity smell which she took to be a mixture of wines and possibly brandy.

"You little bugger," he said in a low, vicious tone. "It's your fault I'm being messed around and put through it, you and your bloody camera. Where was I and what was I doing and have I ever bought this or that and did I want my wife dead? I told them and told them, I loved my wife." His tone changed to one of maudlin self-pity. There was a real tear on his cheek. He was looking at her reproachfully with eyes which just failed to focus. "I'll mourn her till my dying day and so I told them over and over. I was going to take her on that cruise but she decided that she had to go visit her sister. She was like that. Family duty. And generous. She told me to go on the cruise myself. She didn't say take along some slut I met in a pub, someone I never saw before or since, but she wouldn't have cared. It was a nothing, a doesn't-matter. I shouldn't've done it but a man has his needs and she knew that. Then you go and give them a photograph of us and tell the world that was me and the wife."

"You *told* me that she was your wife," Jenny pointed out as calmly as she could manage. "How was I to know that you were lying?"

Mr Oliver was not in a mood for sweet reason. "And now," he said, "there's whispering going about and the police are haunting me and the insurance won't pay up."

"Welcome to the club." Jenny remembered suddenly that she was the injured party. "Did you burn my flat and put me in hospital?" she demanded.

"Is that what happened? I didn't even know. But I can't say I'm sorry." He began to work up a fresh head of indignation. "Interfering guttersnipes deserve worse. I ought to . . . ought . . ."

"You lay one finger on me," Jenny said, "and I'll scream rape. Remember where we are."

He blinked and backed off an inch or two. "They think I killed my wife. Didn't," he said thickly.

"What were you doing at the Westerlink fire?" she asked him.

Indignation gave way to puzzlement. "Just happened by. What's that to do with anything?"

Now that she had asked the question she was unsure what it did have to do with anything. "You listen to me," she said bravely, "or I'll scream rape anyway. You introduce a woman to me as your wife so I let the papers have a photograph of the two of you and then you turn round and start a libel action. And somebody torches my flat and I get burnt and . . . and have to have a skin graft and the insurance won't pay me either and the papers won't touch my photographs and it's all your bloody fault."

He clenched his fists but thought better of it. He began to turn away but she took a deep breath and he turned back again quickly. Jenny let half the breath out again. "Just let me tell you this," she said. "You're a fool. You start a libel action and it's all coming out. You won't just be investigated by an over-committed police force, you'll have the investigative journalists poking into every corner of your life. You won't win against the papers and when you lose it'll cost you every penny your wife left you and more besides. You can't get legal aid to pursue a libel action. Think about that. And then they'll prove what the police can't, that you killed your wife."

She saw the aggression overflow in him again. She would defend herself. Her new trainers were too soft to be used as weapons but she had heard about the effect of a knee in the groin.

He must have sensed her determination. He deflated. "But I didn't," he said.

"You start a libel action and you'll have to prove it," she said. "Are you having me followed?"

"Why in God's name would I do that? I don't know or care where you go or what you do. You can go all the way to hell and back and I wouldn't give a rat's fart."

He swayed a few inches further back and began to turn away again. "You're not planning to drive in your condition, are you?" she demanded. She had a horrid picture in her mind of being landed with an obligation to drive him home. It was the last straw. She felt the tears coming.

He shook his head so violently that he nearly fell down. "Were you thinking of landing me in the shit? Again?" He pointed towards the gates. "I'm in the hotel over there. And it's all your fault," he repeated. "Can't fix myself up until it's all settled."

"Me neither," Jenny said bitterly and with a fine disregard for grammar. She ducked under his outflung arm, resisting the temptation to give him a slap below the belt as she went by, and escaped through the glass door.

The sergeant on desk duty must have been accustomed to young ladies arriving in tears, with much nose-blowing and face-mopping. He pushed within her reach a box of tissues which seemed to be kept on the counter for that very purpose and made an unemotional phone call.

Bob Welles, when he arrived a minute or two later, was at first less impassive. He whisked her into a lift and, as it climbed the tall building, demanded to know what was wrong.

"I met Mr Oliver in the car park."

"And he blames you for his downfall? He was a bit stoned and he didn't take kindly to being questioned again."

"He was awful."

"In a way, you can't blame him. You mustn't let these things get to you. The first lesson a detective learns is to look at things from the other person's point of view. If you're going to—"

Bob broke off short. A moment later the lift stopped. He put an arm round her shoulders (first looking up and down the corridor to be sure that this breach of police etiquette was unobserved) and led her into a vacant room which held four desks. Bob's desk, unlike the others, was very tidy, she noticed, and he himself was comparatively presentable in another polo-neck. He had had his hair cut. They sat on either side of the desk.

"What were you going to say?" she asked.

"Nothing."

"You were. You started saying 'If you're going to—' and then you stopped suddenly."

He frowned, as if at an irrelevance. "Only that if you're going to get uptight every time somebody acts a bit fed up, you're in the wrong profession. News photographers are always being either courted or warded off, never ignored. Here's the cheque for your services to date, by the way."

She still had not acquired a handbag, but the trouser suit had minimal pockets. She folded the cheque and put it away. "That isn't what you were going to say," she told him.

"It's a near enough approximation. And I was going to add that you look fabulous. What was Oliver telling you?"

For a few seconds Jenny lost the thread of the conversation. Then it came back to her. "Like you said, he blames me for everything. And he says that he loved his wife and that they already had the tickets for the cruise when she went off to Australia so she told him to go on his own. And, of course, he didn't. He invited some stray popsy to come along at the last minute, somebody he doesn't know and hasn't seen since, because, he said, a man has his needs. Is that what he told you?"

"Pretty much."

"Well, did you ask him how the booking had been changed to a different name and how they came to have passports as Mr and Mrs Cromwell? It must have been planned some weeks ahead."

Bob glanced involuntarily at the door as if expecting to spy Mr Oliver eavesdropping at the keyhole. "We're saving that up to hit him with later, so keep it under your hat for the moment."

"I promise," Jenny said. "He had to be lying about that and he didn't even sound convincing, it was just what he had to say in the circumstances, but I had the feeling that the rest of what he said could have been true."

Bob swivelled his chair and looked out of the window, high above the rooftops of the city. "We've very little evidence either way as yet. Belief and disbelief don't have a great deal to do with it; what we're looking for is the truth." He turned back again. "But I'll offer you one little titbit. We've been looking for witnesses who saw a stranger approaching our flats before your fire. So far we've only got one sighting that we can't eliminate. And the visitor was a woman. Which may mean anything or nothing."

"Was she fat or thin?" Jenny asked.

"Good question. Unfortunately the witness was changing a wheel at the time. He lives in the flat above mine. He only saw her legs, or else he didn't look any higher. He said that she had rather good legs and was wearing a short tartan skirt. He was adamant that those weren't the legs of any resident in the flats or a regular visitor. He seems to pride himself on being a bit of a connoisseur of legs. He had a few kind words to say about yours, by the way."

"Nice of him!" Jenny paused and considered. She had never noticed the legs of Mrs Oliver-Cromwell. In the photograph taken on the cruise ship the couple's legs were hidden by the table. And, of course, a man's ideal female leg might differ from her own preference. "That doesn't sound like the woman who's been stalking me," she said.

"Not if that one is, as you said, short in the leg. We have an idea who your stalker might be and you needn't worry about her." Bob picked a document from one of an orderly row of trays. "Here's your statement from last night. Read it over and, if you agree with it, sign."

Reading the statement brought it all back. "Were they very hard on you, your bosses?" she asked in a small voice.

He raised his eyebrows. "It isn't the first time a prisoner's escaped from custody. They tore me off a strip but I could see that they thought it was rather funny. Mr Largs, in particular, nearly choked trying not to laugh his head off, but all that he said was that we'd have to spend more on our handcuffs. To make up for my incompetence we've had certain gains. We had our hands on one of the arsonists, we have a good picture of him, we'll soon have him again and we collected valuable evidence against him. The hot-water bottle and your photograph of him trying to get rid of it will be enough to sink him. And, in fact, we've since found out who he is by asking around the probation officers. Unfortunately, he left home some time ago and is thought to be living in a squat somewhere. His name's Tyrone Hayes and he comes of a respectable but single-parent family."

"You're not being disciplined or anything?"

"Good God, no!"

"And you're not still angry with me?"

He laughed aloud and leaned across the desk to pat her hand. "I never was angry with you. Only with myself, for not remembering your cameras and locking the car myself." He sobered. "If I gave you the impression that I was angry with you, then it was clumsy of me and I'm sorry. I'm the one who got it all wrong. You only did the sensible thing."

"Don't be nice to me or I'll start boo-hooing again," she said. She kept her head down, signing her statement.

"I mean it. I should have had the spare key with me. I should have done a dozen things. You did all the right things and it was my fault they turned out to be wrong. All right now?"

She nodded. She looked around. "Much better. So this is where you work."

He looked round as though seeing the room for the first time. "Here and in various incident rooms and out on crime scenes and attending courts and observing post-mortems and making enquiries from door to door and helping with fingertip searches. Anything and anywhere."

"What comes next?" she asked.

He looked at his watch. "Next, I think I take you out and buy you a drink to cheer you up."

"I'll take you up on the kind offer but I meant what comes next in the investigation." She saw that he was laughing at her. "As you very well knew," she added severely.

"Guilty as charged," he said lightly. "Mostly it's a matter of routine. We're still trying to find the so-called Mrs Cromwell but we don't have much to go on and our Mr Oliver remains stubborn."

"Nobody recognises her from my photograph?"

"I wish that were true. The trouble is that everybody recognises her and gives a different identification. We're having to trace and eliminate every thin woman for miles around plus several who have recently lost or gained weight. It all takes time, especially when you remember that she may not live close to here. All the stultifying routine goes on, showing your photograph of the lady to whoever might recognise her, checking with

182

chemists who might remember selling crystals of iodine and so on and so forth."

"What about the boy?"

"He'll have to surface eventually, if only to claim his assistance money – his squat-mates won't want to keep him for ever. And we have one extra card up our sleeves. The firemaster is bringing forward the date for the controlled burning. It's a former warehouse, built almost entirely of timber and long past its sell-by date. We're planning to make an announcement in the papers and have it mentioned on the radio news on Monday morning, on the pretext of asking people not to clog up the telephone lines reporting it to the emergency services. It may draw our young friend out of the woodwork. After all, he seemed very indignant at missing the spectacle yesterday. The psychologists tell us that these firebugs don't care too much who started the blaze, they get their kicks out of watching the pretty flames. And next time, if he shows his face, I won't be so gullible."

It seemed very unlikely to Jenny that the boy had anything to do with her problems, which seemed to derive from the Oliver fire and her own. "I think that woman's still following me," she said. "The one in the grey van. I can't be sure of seeing her, except that I think she followed me into the Castle Hotel this morning, though I didn't think about it until later. But I *feel* watched. Does that make sense?"

"Of a sort, though I've never been quite convinced that anyone can feel eyes on them. I think that any such feeling is due to a recognition of warning signs below the level of consciousness. I've watched enough suspects and if they don't see anything to make them suspicious they stay quite unaware of being watched. Why do you suppose anyone would want to watch you?"

"To see when I'm coming home?"

"Then they'll see me arrive with you. And this time I'll pick up any coins from the carpet. And keep them. And now, let's go and have that drink."

They had their drink and a bar meal. Bob had to return to his report writing but Jenny went home. Bob followed her down the road and cruised once around the block but the only grey van to be seen was large, ancient and delivering furniture.

There was little work to be done about the flat. Jenny was not used to life without television, but the purchase of a telly would be well down her shopping list. She decided to join the local library. She tuned the radio to give her light music as an accompaniment to studying her mobile phone and the leaflet of instructions. She mastered the knack of programming in her most commonly called numbers and she stored the numbers of her parents' house, the *Tidings*, Dan Mandible's number and, when she found that she was running out of regular contacts, Bob's home and mobile numbers. She tested the system on the number of her own home phone and was gratified to be rewarded with a loud ring.

Now that she was in a mood for mastering new challenges, she got out the digital camera and the instruction book that had come with it. She wished that she had had the book with her in hospital, the one occasion when she had ample leisure for study. Until then, she had progressed little further than pointing the device and pressing what on a conventional camera would have been the shutter release. However, when she came to read through the instructions in peace and quiet with the camera and the instruction book in front of her, she found that it took only a little concentration to make sense of the technology. She had so far depended on the simple instructions given by the man in the shop and had lacked the confidence to make use of the camera except as a backup to her other cameras, but a number of those shots were already stored in its digital memory.

One big advantage of the digital system was that frames stored in the camera could be called back up to the viewfinder in order to verify that the subjects had been captured in desired form. She began to scroll through the surprising number of shots stored in the memory. She had heard Bob's returning footsteps in the hall. A few minutes later, she was knocking at his door.

He seemed unsurprised to find her on the doormat. "I've just made tea," he said briskly. "You must have smelled it. Come in. I must go and wash my hands. Take a chair, help yourself to biscuits and things and I'll pour you a cup as soon as it's properly infused." Jenny, unable to get a word in, was pointing at his television and holding up the camera. "You want to take a photograph of my television set?" he asked with an air of puzzlement.

"If you'll pipe down for a minute, stop trying to be funny and listen to me," Jenny said, "I'll explain. This is an electronic, digital camera. I have some shots in it that might interest you, but until I replace my computer and the software I can't make prints. I paid over the odds to get a camera with an extra chip or whatever it is, so that

I can view my shots on any old telly, but without a telly I can't even look properly at what I've got. So I want to plug the camera into your aerial socket and no, I don't want to take a photograph of your hideously ugly telly, thank you very much. Which channel don't you use?"

"Six, seven and eight are vacant." Properly chastened, Bob went to deal with the tea, leaving Jenny to puzzle out the use of the connecting lead and the various sockets.

He returned with a tray laden with all the makings of a vicarage tea party, even to a teacosy. "If I'm going to start entertaining young ladies," he said, "I may as well do it properly."

Jenny congratulated him and told him that he had got it right, doilies and all, except for a cover on the milk jug. "And a curate's delight," she added.

"What on earth's that?"

"That's the thing with three little trays, one above the other, that fold up suddenly when you least expect it and shoot the cream buns onto the carpet." She nearly promised him that he would make somebody an excellent husband some day, but decided against the remark. She accepted a piece of shortbread and tea in a cup with a saucer instead of the customary mug before folding herself down again onto the floor in front of the television. She toyed experimentally with the camera. The TV screen suddenly showed the interior of the shop where she bought the camera followed by several shots of the exterior of the flats and one of the jeep. Then, suddenly, they were outside the Oliver house and scanning the rapt faces of the gathering spectators. Jenny paused. "Good depth of field," she remarked. "Of course, prints from a good printer would be sharper." She scrolled on and stopped at a frame showing the spectators gathering. Bob himself appeared in the foreground but for the moment she ignored his image. She could brood over it some other time. "You see that woman in the headsquare and the pale mackintosh? I'm sure that's the *soi-disant* Mrs Oliver, a.k.a. Cromwell."

"Hm," was all that Bob said, but Jenny could see that his mind was buzzing.

"There's more," she said. She flicked forward five or six frames and found a shot which looked more obliquely along the street. "I thought so," she said triumphantly. "I ruddy well thought so. The woman didn't stick around. Look in the background. She's getting into a car."

"You can't see her face," Bob objected.

"But I'd swear to the mac and headsquare from the earlier shot. You can't quite make it out but the number plate's in full view. If we go and use my brother's facilities . . ."

"No need for that," said Bob quickly. "Let me borrow the camera for our technicians. We'll have that number out of it by breakfast time."

* * *

She heard the phone ring in Bob's flat as she lay in her half-wakened morning doze but by the time she was up and dressed he had gone out. There were no particular demands on her time so she spent the day in the jeep, circling the city and looking for news, or for pictorial material in the hope that her feature would again become regular.

She was seeing the world with new eyes and it seemed

to be well larded with amusing and photogenic subjects. A small man was engaged in a tug-of-war with an enormous St Bernard dog; an even smaller girl was parading round a front garden in some of her mother's clothes and much of her make-up; a sign outside a corner shop read *Closed for re-opening*; and there was a brass band in the park. She fussed around, finding the most telling angle for each shot and making use of the zoom lens to capture her subjects from a distance without making them self-conscious. Twice she glimpsed small grey vans, or possibly the same van twice, but when she tried to pursue one of them it turned two corners and seemed to vanish. When that van or the other one reappeared, she caught it with the telephoto lens. The registration number should be readable on the developed and enlarged photograph.

Late in the afternoon, she found herself at no great distance from the Oliver house and, on a whim, she turned aside and parked the jeep to take another look at the ruin. Some tidying had been done around the garden but otherwise it was the same desolate scene. There was nothing more to be learned. She had turned to go back to the jeep when a voice spoke, as it seemed, out of nowhere.

"Hello there," it said. "I nearly didn't recognise you without your glasses. It was the suit that caught my attention."

A bosomy lady with a round face and carefully sculpted hair rose from behind a low screen of rhododendrons. She had secateurs in one hand and a trug of dead flower heads in the other. Jenny recognised her friend from the charity shop.

"I've gone back to my contact lenses," Jenny said. "Hi, there. That's an awful mess you have next door to you."

"Isn't it just! And we can't find out when anything's going to be done about it."

A moment's calculation assured Jenny that the lady must have been the good neighbour who had led Mr Oliver away after the fire and that she would probably have been at the charity shop when Jenny had been at the scene with Bob and the other investigators. "I saw Mr Oliver yesterday," she said with perfect truth. "He said that he couldn't get any sense out of his insurers. I believe you took him in after the fire?"

Those statements seemed to constitute a social introduction. The lady held out her hand. "I'm Mrs Congreve," she said.

"Jenny Ambleton."

They shook hands.

"I was just going to give up and go in for a cup of tea," Mrs Congreve said. "Would you like one?"

"Love one."

"Splendid! My husband's away and the boys are at football, so I was beginning to get sick of my own company."

"Just give me a moment to lock the car."

Ten minutes later they were established in a spacious and well-equipped kitchen in surprisingly comfortable dining chairs. Earl Grey was served in bone-china cups. "You'll have to excuse being entertained in the kitchen," Mrs Congreve said, "but I can't get the smell of smoke out of the sitting room. I've sent the curtains and covers for dry cleaning and they're coming to shampoo the carpet next week."

"That should do it."

"It should do, what it's costing. How do you come to know David Oliver?"

The truth still seemed to be the best form of lie. "We met on a cruise ship last winter," Jenny said, "and occasionally since."

Mrs Congreve looked mildly amused. "While Jane was in Australia. Did you meet his . . . companion?"

Jenny pretended shock. "He introduced her as his wife. Wasn't she? I thought that the lady I met aboard must have been the one who died in the fire."

Her hostess shook her head and looked coy.

"Oh dear!" Jenny said. "I hope his wife never found out. I'd hate to think of her being miserable in her last weeks."

It seemed that Mrs Congreve was in the mood for a good gossip. "My dear," she said, "Jane would never have minded. They were a very close couple at one time, still lovebirds. In those days, yes, she'd have been bitterly hurt. But she was a few years older than he was and when she came to a certain age . . . Things happen to a woman. You know? The change?"

"So I've heard."

"Sex became quite painful for her, she told me. Of course, you can get artificial lubricants but she reacted badly to the first one they tried and after that . . . David started his womanising and Jane told me quite frankly that she was relieved. They were still fond of each other, but he looked elsewhere for his nooky and she was quite happy with her house and garden."

"So who was the woman I met on the ship?" Jenny asked.

"I've no idea. He was very discreet about his little affairs. In fact, I think he was under the impression that nobody knew about them, especially Jane."

She returned home in the early evening, hungry and depressed that Mr Oliver's guilt seemed to be becoming ever more remote. She was preparing to make a meal when Bob knocked on the door. "You can come in," Jenny said, "provided it's understood that I'm hungry so I'm not going to stand on ceremony. I'm going to cook and eat on my knee and nobody's going to stop me. You can join me if you like and we'll talk about anything but fires until after we've eaten."

"I like," Bob said. "And I'll contribute something to the feast. But why don't you come and cook it in my kitchen? I have a table and chairs," he added as an inducement.

So Jenny cooked a double-sized omelette in Bob's kitchen and Bob contributed cheese and onion to the omelette, strawberries and cream to follow and white wine from a cardboard box.

They sat down to eat in perfect accord. When the edge was off her hunger, Jenny said, "Now you can tell me how it went today. Still in confidence, I promise."

Bob took two more quick mouthfuls and put his fork down. "You were quite right," he said. "The car's number plate came up quite legibly with the right equipment. The DVLA at Swansea confirmed that the number belonged to the same make of car and gave us the name of the keeper – which turned

191

out to be Mr Oliver's garden centre and landscaping firm."

"Oho!" said Jenny.

"Le mot juste," said Bob. "So, you see, you're not the only one who can break into French occasionally. Oho, indeed! We now had enough to turn Mr Oliver inside out, at which Mr Largs is highly skilled. He dished it out, one piece at a time. Oliver first acted surprised that we should think anything of one of his firm's cars being seen near his house. Then, when the identity of the lady was mooted, he said that she had been buying a car and had asked him to see to the registration for her; and, because her marriage had broken up and she did not have a permanent address at the time, he had used his own business address for the purpose. He still insisted that the lady was and became again a stranger to him. At that point, he was asked your question – how it was that the bookings were made and passports obtained, all in false names, in ample time if, as he maintained, he met her for the first time a day or two before sailing."

"To which he wittily replied?"

"At which he gobbled and ran out of lies altogether, asked for his solicitor and then cancelled the request and generally acted like a man who's about to come clean. He admitted that he had known her for some time and had caught her on the rebound from an unsatisfactory marriage on her part. He expressed himself as very penitent at having been unfaithful to his wife, but he insisted that the affair meant nothing to him and that he had no idea where she had moved to after quitting the family home. We checked as much of the story as was checkable and found it to be more or less the truth;

but whether he really does not know where she is now is open to question. We're trying to keep a discreet eye on him, insofar as manpower will allow. Maybe he'll lead us to her."

"And maybe he's guilty," Jenny said without much hope, "and using her as a red herring."

"Maybe. But, frankly, I don't think he's as clever as that. Many people are only intelligent over a small area and quite successful businessmen often turn out to have the common sense of a gerbil."

Jenny still refused to abandon her determination that Mr Oliver had to be guilty. Too much hung on it. "Well, you should know. But, looking at the picture as a whole, it doesn't seem to me that there's somebody very clever at the back of it. Or somebody too clever for their own good. I mean," she said seriously, "that somebody could easily have faked an accidental fire or rigged it to look as though the other arsonist had started both the Oliver fire and mine, but he was too ingenious about rigging his booby traps. So what happens now?"

"Routine continues," Bob said. "And the controlled burning goes ahead on Monday and we'll be keeping a watchful eye out. Will you be there?"

"Probably. I can't expect to have the scene to myself, but if there's any hope of an arrest being made I'll be there with my journalist's hat on."

"I've never seen you in a hat," Bob said. "Leave the dishes, I'll see to them."

Ten

The controlled burning was scheduled for the Monday afternoon – time enough, as Bob explained, for the news to break in the *Tidings* and local radio but not long enough, it was hoped, to allow young Mr Hayes to develop cold feet or to forget his frustration at being robbed of the previous spectacle. Bob promised to meet Jenny at the site. "Bring sandwiches," he said. "We may have to wait around."

Dutifully, Jenny spent Sunday with her family, telling them as much as she thought was good for them and evading questions about Bob Welles. Her mother tried to force on her all the calories that the good lady was sure she must have missed since leaving home. Her father again offered financial help but his heart was clearly not in it and, though tempted, Jenny again declined. She herself, she had decided, could not lose what she did not have. If she was going to be smitten by financial disaster, a firm barrier between her finances and those of the family might be wisest.

She heard Bob come in late that evening and go out again early. He was still not to be seen when Jenny, after a morning spent waiting at the zoo for the birth of a lion cub which turned out to be stillborn, reached

194

the site of the controlled burning. The warehouse, an ancient structure of largely timber construction and cladding, stood alone in a wasteland of demolition, in the middle of a site destined, according to the *Tidings*, for a major redevelopment of shops and offices. She parked inconspicuously where she would not be obstructing the fire crews nor, she hoped, getting smokestains on her washed and polished jeep.

A single fire appliance was standing by. Fire officers were already fussing in and out of the building and soon the first smoke was followed by visible flames. The spectacle did not attract the same crowds as an unintentional fire and Jenny concluded that for the average, unfixated rubberneck, the fascination of watching somebody else's property go up in smoke was the missing element. She wandered around, out of habit, photographing the watching faces and recorded a panoramic strip of the temporarily exposed buildings, ancient and modern, surrounding the area at a distance. For the rest of the time, she sat in the jeep and watched them come and go. The blaze mounted. Several constables circled the building to make sure that the few spectators stayed out of danger.

A photographer from the *Tidings*, not Charlie but one who had lectured on her course, arrived and took a few shots. He paused for a chat as one professional to another. He was carrying the latest digital video camera, his personal possession with which, he explained, he could take a lengthy sequence and later pick out the most suitable frames, while there was always the option of selling the moving sequence to television. He departed, leaving Jenny in a fresh agony of yearning.

Half-way through the afternoon her new mobile phone sounded. Jenny was not accustomed to its note and took it for a nearby starling on a phone wire. When she recognised the sound and managed to find the instrument and its pickup button, Bob was calling. "I'll be with you shortly," he said. "Keep an eye out for the woman. If you see her, point her out to the nearest bobby."

"Which woman?"

"Either of them," Bob said, with only a moment's hesitation.

"Will do. There's no sign of the young man," Jenny said.

"There wouldn't be. We've caught him. See you."

Fifteen minutes later, a white police car decanted him beside the jeep. The officer at the wheel winked at her before driving off. Bob settled into the seat beside her and handed back her digital camera.

"I think that the woman who's been watching me was here an hour ago," Jenny said. "She buzzed off as soon as she saw that I'd spotted her."

"Same little grey van?"

"No. This time it was a dusty red Fiesta. There's been no sign of Mrs Oliver-Cromwell, unless she's another mistress of disguise."

Bob took a proffered sandwich but delayed starting to eat. "It was almost too much to hope for," he said, "but one must go through the motions. We know who she is, now."

"The woman who's been spying on me?"

"No, the other one. The suspect. She's one Agnes Murcatt, née Burbage, a former teacher and now a divorcee, for all the good it does us. I spent most of

196

yesterday and some of today following up a false lead to where she might be now. Then young Hayes was picked up by an observant copper who'd seen and remembered your photograph. His mother came and raised the roof – her boy wouldn't do anything like that and anyway it wasn't his fault it was all because his father had walked out when he was only three – none of which was any of my business. When the solicitor she got for him heard and saw the evidence that we've stacked up he decided to head towards a plea of diminished responsibility. He may be able to make it stick."

"If I read about a psychiatric hospital being burned down, I'll know that he did make it stick," Jenny said.

"Yes. In the meantime," Bob said with his mouth full, "the young man had admitted setting the fires, all but Mr Oliver's and yours."

Jenny gave a sigh which spattered crumbs onto the dashboard. She got busy with a tissue. "Sorry about that, but those are the two that I need to see solved. All my worries will be over if you can nail either Mr Oliver or the woman for them. I still haven't heard from Norfolk General."

Bob was slow to answer. He ate a whole sandwich and drank some tea. He was obviously deep in thought. Jenny waited respectfully. "You will, I still promise you," he said at last. "We're probably wasting our time here. The way I read it, somebody saw one or more of Tyrone Hayes's fires and got ideas. But that doesn't meant that they caught his pyromania, just that they realised what a good way a fire is to solve a problem and at the same time cover up the evidence."

"It doesn't mean that they're *not* equally pyromaniacal,

if there is such a word," Jenny said. "I first met Mr Oliver at the Westerlink fire."

"And photographed the woman at the Oliver fire," Bob pointed out. "And that doesn't necessarily mean a thing either."

The day wore on. They finished Jenny's sandwiches and the thermos of tea and argued about the meaning of life, the real difference between men and women and why fish, which could easily have supported heavy brains in their weightless environment, aren't cleverer than people. The warehouse roof fell in, sending cascades of sparks up into the darkening clouds. The fire began to dwindle.

"But suppose," Bob said suddenly, "that neither of those two turns out to be guilty?"

"Then," Jenny said, "I may still be up the proverbial creek without even a proverbial paddle, if the media decide to pay Mr Oliver the compensation he's after."

"He won't press it," said Bob.

"He might. Can't you frame one of them? I thought the police were supposed to be good at – what do they call it? – *fitting up* a suspect."

Bob snorted with laughter. He gave her a friendly punch on the shoulder which she returned with interest. "If you're going to . . . to believe all you read in the tabloids," he said, "you'll believe in Santa Claus."

"I *do* believe in Santa Claus. Bob," Jenny said, "once before, in your office, you started to say what you said just now – 'If you're going to—' and you stopped suddenly."

"The lift had reached my floor."

"No, it hadn't. Not quite. You stopped yourself from saying something. You were sort of intense. I don't like people who start to say things and then change their minds. It suggests a secretive nature or a vacillating one. What were you going to say?"

"Something that I've decided to save until you're a little older."

Jenny sat in silence for a count of ten. "There," she said. "I'm a little older now. What was it?"

Bob chuckled. He turned in his seat to look at her. "I'll tell," he said. "If you really want to know."

"Oh, I do."

"I was about to say that if you're going to be a copper's wife you'll have to stop worrying about a little bit of aggravation now and again."

Jenny was again silenced for a full ten seconds. "You thought that I was too young to hear that?"

"Not really," Bob said frankly. "That was your mother's contribution. She knew from the moment she first saw us together. So did DI Largs."

"I could have betted on him," Jenny said indignantly. "Does nobody mind their own damn business any more? And am I going to be a copper's wife?"

He put an arm round her shoulders. "Yes. Of course. Definitely."

"We haven't known each other very long."

"That's what your mother said. I told her that I knew my mind almost as soon as she did."

"I don't want to nit-pick, but shouldn't you be asking me, not telling me?"

Bob began to withdraw his arm but she caught his hand. "I rather thought that it was understood," he said.

"All the same, it's nice to be asked."

"Perhaps. Now that you put the thought into my mind. Jenny, will you marry me?"

"You could be taking on my debts if Mr Oliver's innocent and goes on making trouble," Jenny pointed out.

"I'll risk it. Will you?"

"Damn silly question," Jenny said. "Yes, of course I will."

Jenny had always found that being kissed by a man was a tiresome and scratchy experience, to be endured rather than enjoyed, but now she wondered how she could have been so wrong. It was exciting. It was loving. It was leading onward . . . "No, not here," she said quickly as he tried to take her fully into his arms. "At home. Your place or mine?"

Bob pulled back and looked at her. "You've done this before."

"Silly! I heard somebody say that in a film once. It seemed like a sophisticated line. I've been waiting for a chance to use it."

The sun was getting low. The firefighters were damping down the last of the fire. The onlookers had vanished and the jeep was isolated in a sea of nothingness. Jenny started the engine. "Where's your car?" she asked.

"Still at the back of HQ. Never mind it. Hurry home. I love you too much to wait."

Jenny could not find a simple answer to that, so she hurried. She parked in front of the building and carried her case into Bob's flat. "Not yet," she said urgently. She set up the Pentax on his mantelpiece and pressed the delay lever. "Now," she said.

The flash was intended to capture their first kiss for the family album, or if not in truth quite the first they could have claimed later that it was their first kiss. Instead, it caught them both looking at the telephone, their annoyance and frustration clearly recorded.

Oh well, Jenny thought. As an opening to the family album it would at least be a talking point. They could try again. And again.

Bob said, "I'd better take it."

Jenny, on the point of saying, "Take me instead," knew that the mood was spoiled. It would come again. She just nodded. Without releasing her, Bob reached out and picked up the phone. His body was hard against hers. With their heads close together, they could both hear the voice clearly.

"DS Welles? You were to be notified of any fires of questionable origin. Fire has just been reported at Fisk's Hotel. It seems to have started simultaneously in several places including a staircase and one of the bedrooms. The Fire Service is suspicious and notified us immediately. That's all we know so far, except that we can see it from the window. Looks bad."

"I'm on my way," Bob said. He let go of Jenny. "That's where Oliver's been living. Lend me your car."

Jenny had no intention of being left behind. She still had the keys in her hand but she kept her fist clenched. "It's only insured for me to drive."

"I'm insured to drive other cars."

"Only third party," Jenny said. It was an argument which members of her family had been in the habit of using against each other. "You can borrow it if you write me out a letter indemnifying me against any damage, however caused, and—"

Bob was hopping with impatience. "All *right*," he said. "Come along, then. God, what a wife you'll make!"

Jenny panted after him with her heavy camera case banging against her leg. "You wouldn't want a wife who lent her car to any Tom, Dick or Harry," she gasped.

Bob grabbed the case from her and almost threw it into the back of the jeep. "Just get us there *quickly*."

Jenny, whose exuberant mood was standing up to the excitement, took this to be an official permit to ignore such irrelevancies as speed limits and red lights. Luckily the streets were quiet and other drivers were cautious, but even so Bob's knuckles were white and he was treading on imaginary brakes before they climbed the last hill and neared the hotel.

"Fisk Street will be a logjam," Bob said. "Park at the front of Police HQ."

Jenny did as suggested. Her Pentax was still on Bob's mantelpiece but she grabbed the digital camera out of her case and locked the jeep. Bob had already vanished through the wide glass doors. Jenny was wearing her new trouser suit but on her feet she wore her red trainers, admirably suited to running. She dashed after him, almost caught him in the long hall, banged through the glass doors with due care for her camera and overtook him in the large car park at the rear. There was a shroud of smoke overhead and a whiff of burning plastic came to meet them.

He turned his head without slowing. "Oliver's staying here," he said. "Too much coincidence?"

"Yes, but why?"

"That's for us to puzzle out."

His forecast was proved accurate. Fisk Street was

occupied by three fire appliances and a number of jammed-in cars. An overflow of people was milling around, obstructing the firefighters and spilling into the police car park. The gate-keeper had given up as a bad job.

Fisk's Hotel occupied the oldest building in the city, a genuine Tudor structure in black and white. The proprietors, Jenny remembered, had been granted a relaxation of the building regulations, which would otherwise have required ugly fire escapes all over the outside of a building which was one of the city's few tourist attractions. Instead, escape reels had been permitted and several of these had been used, judging by the tails and straps still dangling from wide-open windows. Ladders were erect from two of the fire appliances and from the top of each a firefighter was directing water into the windows. Other hoses were spouting from ground level. It looked to Jenny as though any rescues had been either completed or abandoned. Gouts of livid smoke billowed from the upper windows and flames were licking out, staining the white plaster with soot.

They slowed. "A fire trap, Grade One," Bob said.

Some sort of order had been quickly imposed. Escapees from the hotel were being shepherded towards a woman in a dark suit and white blouse, very crisp and businesslike, who had rescued the register and was ticking off names. A fire officer was looking over her shoulder. As they came up, she said, "All the staff are accounted for and all but five of the guests. A party of four is still to come back from the theatre and supper."

"And the other?" the fire officer asked.

"A Mr Oliver. He went up early. Frankly, he was well under the influence and a bottle had been sent up to his room. He was in Two-one-four. That's the top right-hand corner of the building as you look at it. That's where the worst of the fire started." She closed the register with a loud snap. Her voice was matter-of-fact. Her face was grim but it was not for her to arrive at any conclusions.

The fire officer squinted up at the building. "Hopeless! You're sure that that's the lot?"

"Unless any of the guests had guests of their own in their rooms. I mightn't know about that." She looked with disfavour at a young woman who was still struggling into a tight dress behind the back of an elderly and very embarrassed man in a brocade dressing gown.

The fire officer was only momentarily distracted by this by-play. "You're supposed to have a sprinkler system," he said severely.

"It was being replaced and modernised – on your boss's recommendation. They were supposed to finish last week but they were waiting for parts, they said."

Jenny had been looking around, absorbing the scene prior to taking photographs. She grabbed Bob by the sleeve. "Don't scare her off," she said, "but look over my shoulder. The woman coming from the police building. Blue mac, pale trousers and long black hair. See her?"

"I see her," Bob said.

"That's the woman who's been following me around. I'd know that waddle anywhere."

"Leave this to me." Looking straight ahead, Bob set off on an oblique course from which he could make a curve to intercept the woman. Jenny moved away. She could hear it all later from Bob. Meantime, she had another job to do. Charlie, from the *Tidings*, was already there but Dan had told her never to let the presence of other photo-journalists deter her from taking her own shots, citing, among others, a case in which the first photographer on the scene had later found that his camera had not been winding on. There would be time later to find out about her stalker, time also to enquire about Mr Oliver and to mourn him if nobody else cared to do it. She had heard somewhere that relatives could not make a libel claim on behalf of somebody who had died, but she would think about that later. Making a record came first.

She took one or two general shots, but the onlookers had their backs to her and she wanted faces. To the right of the hotel was a drive to the hotel's rear car park, but to the right again of the drive was a block of lockup garages running back from the road. A planning department, for once acting with discretion and common sense, had prevented the hotel's owners from defacing the Tudor frontage and so, instead, the end wall of the garages abutting on Fisk Street had been doubled in height as a sort of false gable to form a backdrop and support for the hotel's neon sign. From where she stood, Jenny could recognise the perfect viewpoint and photographic platform.

Taking advantage of a confused eddy of rescued and rescuers, she managed to detour around the guarding constables and crossed Fisk Street. Behind the garages, the ground rose sharply to a strip of waste ground covered by weeds. Somebody had placed a dustbin against the back of the garages and from this it would be an easy step to the roofs.

She was not the first to seek this vantage point. The backs of half a dozen figures were ranged in silhouette in front of her. Even as she considered and rejected the idea of joining them she realised that she had an ideal composition in front of her. Midsummer daylight had persisted, the sun had found some gaps in the clouds but now the light was going and the mixture of rose-tinted, almost horizontal sunshine, street and vehicle lights and the glare of the flames lit the scene and the smoke above in a way that might have been an inspired set-designer's vision for an enactment of Dante's *Inferno*. Even the clouds had piled themselves into sculptural forms. Through the frieze of figures in front of her could be seen the hotel, the timber structure and shingle roof now well alight and defying the shining jets of water. And below were the faces of the onlookers, relishing the drama and the destruction.

As the figures in the foreground moved and the flames grew brighter, Jenny busied herself in capturing variations on the theme. The digital camera was far more tolerant of poor lighting conditions than a camera using conventional film. Her concentration was total, so she was startled when she realised that a young policeman was standing behind her. She wondered if he had been there, perhaps admiring the lower part of her figure, for some time. Or perhaps not. "You people come down off there," he said loudly. "You're not safe. That roof could give way."

"It feels quite solid," said a man's voice.

"Those are corrugated asbestos-cement sheets," said

the policeman, who seemed to know what he was talking about. "Brittle. It could go suddenly. Or the gable could come down on you."

"It couldn't reach this far," said a woman.

The policeman might be young and he had a thin and sensitive face. Jenny thought that he would probably not survive for long in the stressful world of policing, but he was not going to be messed about. "Think what you like," he said grimly, "but come down here or I'll call for back-up to remove you. Then you'll face a summons."

Jenny opened her mouth to protest. She closed it again. Something in the shadows had caught her eye. She decided to gamble on her luck, for Bob's sake. She got down from the dustbin. Grumbling, four men and two women used it to descend to the sloping ground. The policeman ushered them all back to the police car park.

Jenny was suddenly in a fever pitch of impatience. She looked around but in the milling crowd she could not see Bob. She had her new mobile phone in her pocket and with luck he would be similarly equipped. She keyed in the short code for Bob's mobile number and got a double tone. Somewhere his mobile phone was sounding, but was it in his pocket, his flat or his car? To her relief, he answered on the seventh tone.

"Meet me behind the hotel garages," she said, "or as near as we can get. And hurry. This isn't an assignation. I think it may be the answer to all our prayers." While she spoke she watched the back of the garages but no more figures came climbed down.

"Coming," Bob said briefly. "And you may care to know that the lady stalking you is a private investigator."

Jenny was moving again. She had to push through a forest of figures, all wandering without apparent purpose, but the hubbub of noise was quite enough to screen her words. Somehow what Bob had said seemed impossible. "A what?"

"A private eye. A snooper. A shamus."

"I thought they died out when the divorce laws changed."

"Who do you think digs up evidence for a defence in a criminal trial? She tried to plead client confidentiality, but that doesn't apply in this country. When I showed her a pair of handcuffs, she decided to spill the beans. The Norfolk General Branch Manager hired her, at his own personal expense."

Jenny was back at the gate. The young policeman was fifty yards away, harassing some teenagers who had been climbing the fence for a better view of the fire. She slipped outside again. "What on earth for?" she said.

"Hoping to catch you out doing a bit of fire-raising on your own account. I gather that he was already under investigation. He was suspended yesterday. He's suspected of putting through false claims, so his neck's on the block. Attempting to balance the books by rejecting your perfectly valid claim would be the last straw and the only thing to save him would be if he could prove that he was right all along."

It was too much to absorb all at once. "Come quick," Jenny said. They disconnected.

Jenny followed the route that she had taken earlier, detouring around policemen and firefighters. The young constable had moved the dustbin back from the garages but it took her only a moment to replace and mount it. She breathed a great sigh of relief. The figure was still there. The constable's view had been from a lower viewpoint than hers and had been partially obscured by her body. Stock-still, and tucked into the black shadows cast by the heightened end wall of the garages, she had seen another figure, rapt in admiration of the flames.

She looked to the side. Nothing. She waited and looked again. Bob's sturdy shape was approaching from the direction of the fire appliances. The short-legged figure of the private detective was struggling to keep up with him. It was time to speak.

"You seem to be losing your lover," she said loudly.

The woman glanced over her shoulder and then turned again to the spectacle. "Don't call him that," she said. Her voice was harsh, not the honeyed tones that Jenny remembered from the cruise ship. She had to raise it almost to a shout to be heard above the roar and crackle. "He never loved me, whatever he said. I was just a convenient body when his wife was away."

"Men are like that," Jenny said. Arriving beside her, Bob gave a grunt of disagreement.

"That bastard certainly was. Him and my husband, a right pair of bookends they'd have made. One goes off with a masseuse half his age but the other . . . goes back to his wife, would you believe? As long as she was away, he kept telling me that his marriage was breaking up, but that we had to choose the right time for a split because she held the purse-strings. It was any old excuse to put off committing himself, I can see that now. When she came back, he tried to fob me off with a tale about the sanctity of marriage and all that balls, but when I threatened to tell his wife he said . . . awful things." There was a pause, as though the woman was waiting to be asked what things. When the question was not asked, she went on. "The worst was that he'd been preparing all along to let me down. When I worked for him he fixed it so that I'd seem to have been robbing the firm. If I went near his wife, he said, he'd hand me over to the police. And he admitted that he'd loved his wife all along. I reminded him that that was the opposite of what he'd told me earlier and –" her voice rose to a screech "– what do you think he said?"

"What did he say?" Jenny asked in spite of herself.

The woman's voice dropped until Jenny had to strain to make out the words. "He said, 'What else would I tell you?' – as if it was the only thing to say. Can you believe it? It's her money he loved and now that he's got it he doesn't need me either. And the bitch must have been about a hundred years old. Some kind of love!" she finished scornfully and fell silent.

"So you burnt him," Bob said.

Jenny moved to hush him, but the woman was speaking again, quite audibly now that her shame was out. "He was drunk out of his mind," she said. "Maundering on about how he missed his wife and he'd never love again."

The young constable made another appearance. "I thought I told you–– Oh!" he said. "It's DS Welles, isn't it?"

"Stay where you are," Bob said. "Don't interfere but memorise every word, all of you."

Jenny glanced round. The private investigator had a notebook in her hand and was scribbling frantically, angling her book to catch the available light.

"Did you have to burn my flat?" Jenny asked the woman on the roof. "Did you have to burn *me*? Didn't you know that it was already too late?"

The woman turned and walked towards them up the slope of the roof. A corner of the hotel fell in and in the sudden glare Jenny saw for the first time that the woman had a bottle in her hand. There was spittle on her chin, which caught the light of the flames and looked like blood. Her eyes were unnaturally wide. She stared at Jenny for a moment. "It's you," she said. Her voice was slurring. "I don't care what happens to you. It would have been all right if you hadn't given them that photograph. That's when it all began to go wrong." She turned back towards the flames. Jenny took a shot of her silhouette against the fiery background. They could feel the heat on their faces.

"Where did you get a fresh supply of chlorate?" Bob asked. "From David Oliver's garden centre?"

"Who cares? I like gardening."

Bob sighed. The woman was talking without directly answering his questions. "But you don't have a garden. Your lover tried to keep your identity from us but he cracked in the need. You didn't kill him soon enough. You were staying away from home and we just couldn't find you. We did find where you bought the ammonia. We've spoken to two of your brothers. They admit that when you were all young they taught you the trick with the ammonium iodide."

"Anyone can buy ammonia. You can't prove a damn thing." The woman took a long drink from her bottle. Against the light the liquid was clear – gin or vodka, Jenny thought.

"I think we will," Bob said. "We only have to show your photograph to chemist's assistants and we'll find where you bought the iodine crystals."

"You'll be lucky! I bought them on some island in the Caribbean."

Jenny heard Bob let out a long breath. It was the first real admission and the woman seemed unaware of it. "We have a photograph of you at the scene of the fire in which Mrs Oliver died," he said.

"So? That's no crime. I like watching fires. They have more passion than people. They cleanse. They get rid of the rubbish. That's what this one's doing." She drank again. She was holding a private wake, for her lover and for her dreams.

"Did you stay to watch," Jenny asked, "when you burnt my flat? That must have been a disappointment."

The woman hesitated and decided to be cautious. "I don't know what you're talking about. Either of you. You keep asking me things I know nothing about."

"We have a witness who saw you go into the flats," Bob said. "Do you think he'll be able to pick you out of an identity parade?"

The gable of the hotel collapsed with a crash and a huge uprush of flame. A big timber, showering sparks, pitch-poled across the drive and slammed into one of the garage doors. There was a flicker in the shadows as the faces of the watchers turned towards the new excitement. The suddenly increased heat reminded Jenny of her burns and she jumped down from the dustbin. But the woman only took half a pace back. She seemed to be exulting in the destruction.

The constable woke up to his responsibilities. "Sorry,

Sarge," he said, "but I've a job to do. You must come down, madam. One of the cars could go up at any moment."

"Sod off," said the woman.

"But I bet you had to buy more iodine to do the hotel," said Bob.

The woman laughed raucously. She lurched but regained her balance. "Didn't have to," she said. "Just laid a trail of chlorate down the stairs and dropped a match."

Jenny looked round. The PI's pencil was still racing over the paper.

"Somebody'll have seen you."

"Nobody saw me. The place was sleeping."

The constable was a worthy prophet. The burning timber had stove in a garage door. A petrol tank suddenly erupted, sending a screen of flame to billow up from the front of the roof. The heat must have been almost intolerable but the woman ignored it. "Nobody saw me," she repeated. She had to shout to make herself heard above the flames. Hoses were being directed onto the flames below but they were having no effect.

"Come down," the constable shouted. " Come down at once. The roof—"

"Asbestos doesn't burn."

"It can shatter with heat. Come *down*."

"You're just trying to lure me so that—"

Bob tried to climb onto the dustbin, to drag her off the roof, but Jenny clung to him and pulled him back.

The roof fell in without warning and flames leaped at the sky. The woman vanished without adding a sound to the uproar. Jenny heard, above the din, a whoop as every member of the crowd let out a cry.

They retreated, backing away beyond the reach of that excruciating heat towards where they could hear each other.

"Oh my God!" said the constable. He sounded close to tears. He fumbled with his personal radio.

"You did all you could," Bob said. "Now just concentrate on remembering. Write it down as soon as you can. Your evidence will be needed at two inquests."

Bob and Jenny set off back towards their cars through the maze of wandering hoses and milling firefighters. An ambulance was belling its way through the mêlée although Jenny thought that there were no injured to collect, only the very, very dead. There was a babbling in the crowd as versions of the incident were bandied around. A woman was crying with shock and being comforted, but most of the bystanders were treating the incident as if it had been choreographed for their entertainment.

The woman investigator hurried after them, her short legs working hard to keep up. She was demanding to know who was going to pay for her time and expenses. Bob paused in his stride. "You have a client," he said sharply. "Bill him, and the best of luck. But if you come into court and deny hearing what you heard tonight, I'll have you for perjury."

They left behind the organised chaos of the fire scene. In the peaceful hallway of the police building he stopped again. "You go home," he said gently. "You'll have to make a statement, but tomorrow will be time enough. I must go upstairs and make my report and start a search for her car. It must be somewhere around and we can find evidence in it. You're all right?"

"I'll get by," Jenny said. But when she reached her car she found that her legs were shaking. She drove home slowly and with great care. Sleep seemed to be a very long way away. She sat with a pad on her knee and began to draft a report but the effort was too much after such a day. She remembered suddenly to download the digital camera and send her shots over the wire to Dan Mandible. Then, for lack of anything better to do, she went to bed. From time to time the shakes came again.

She was still awake when she heard Bob return, long after midnight. She had left her door slightly open and she called to him. His dark figure loomed in the light of the street lamps diffused through the curtains.

"Come and hold me," she said. "Nothing more. It'll all happen some other time but, for tonight, just hold me. You can do that?"

"I can do that," he said.